Hands of
DELIVERANCE

Hands of DeLiveRance

Jake & Luke Thoene

THOMAS NELSON PUBLISHERS®
Nashville

Copyright © 2000 by Jake and Luke Thoene

Published in association with the literary agency of Alive Communications, 7680 Goddard Street, Suite #200, Colorado Springs, CO 80920.

Scripture quotations are from THE NEW KING JAMES VERSION. Copyright © 1979, 1980, 1982, Thomas Nelson, Inc., Publishers.

Published in Nashville, Tennessee, by Thomas Nelson, Inc.

Library of Congress Cataloging-in-Publication Data
ISBN 0-7852-7147-3

Printed in the United States of America
1 2 3 4 5 6 QPV 06 04 03 02 01 00

To our sister, Rachel—
many thanks for adding
a woman's heart to
this story.

PROLOGUE

---◈---

June 22, 1807

The bowsprit of the United States frigate *Chesapeake* rose to meet the Atlantic swell as it exited Chesapeake Bay. One of the six new warships of the class built to increase the might and pride of the U.S. fleet, *Chesapeake* had only recently filled her roster. Bearing the broad pennant of Commodore Barron, she was part of the fledgling nation's steps toward respectful treatment in the wider world. As such there had been no shortage of men eager to volunteer in her service.

Like the lift of the waves, pride also exalted the heart of George Washington Canfield, freedman of Baltimore and till last week able-bodied seaman on the French ship *Argus*. *Argus* and other vessels of the navy of Emperor Napoleon were trapped in the neutral harbor of Annapolis by a blockading British force. Canfield and four more American-born sailors, having no desire to rot onboard a ship that might never sail, deserted the hapless French and signed on with Commodore Barron.

In his hometown Canfield still had to carry proof of his free status to avoid being taken up as a runaway slave. This constant harassment had fueled his desire to see other places and to prove he was as good a citizen as any of white skin. Black men were refused permission to enlist in the army of the United States, but the color bar did not apply at sea. Canfield was a skilled woodworker and was instantly accepted as carpenter's mate aboard the *Chesapeake*.

The frigate was passing Norfolk Roads when the foremast lookout raised the cry of "On deck, there! Sail ho!"

"Where away?"

"Two points on the starboard bow."

There was no alarm at this cry; the bay being one of the busiest channels in America, providing as it did sea links to Baltimore and the nation's capital at Washington. Traders, oyster dredges, and visiting warships used the highway of the Chesapeake.

The five-foot-ten-inch Canfield, as one of those who stood day watches, should have been in the cramped carpenter's space on the lowest deck. But this early in the voyage there were no repairs to be done, and he was above in the sun when further information drifted from aloft: "On deck there! She's a British frigate. Looks to be the *Leopard*."

H.M.S. Leopard was one of the blockading vessels keeping the French bottled up.

Commodore Barron strode on deck. A few minutes passed, sailing on the light breeze, and then the dull report of a signal gun thumped the hull of the *Chesapeake*. Barron's demand for the lookout's attention crossed in midair with the cry of "She's breaking out a signal."

The signal flags fluttering from the British rigging requested that the *Chesapeake* heave-to for a parley. The sails backed, the American frigate glided to a halt as her opposing number sailed to within hail and lowered a boat. "What's your business?" Canfield heard Barron inquire of the Royal Navy lieutenant who stood ramrod-straight in the launch. "A despatch for the commodore," was the reply.

The slim English officer in the full fig of his number one uniform wasted no time in relaying the message. "Captain's compliments, Commodore," the lieutenant said tersely. "We have orders to search your ship for deserters. You will muster your crew for my inspection."

"What!" Barron thundered. "By whose authority?"

"Vice-Admiral Berkeley, commander of the North American station, sir."

"You may sail back to Halifax with this message for Lord High-and-Mighty Berkeley," Barron roared. "No one musters my crew but me or my officers. You may play the schoolmaster with trading vessels, but not with a warship of a sovereign power. Be off with you, sir, you and your impertinence, before I have you thrown over the side!"

"Sir," the lieutenant replied, "before you adopt so hasty a . . ."

"Bosun!" Barron ordered. "Escort this gentleman to his launch."

Chesapeake's sails were set, and she was moving forward again before the English officer had been rowed halfway back to *Leopard*. Even before that the drumroll of "Beat to quarters!" was chasing Canfield toward his battle station on the gun deck.

Number-three cannon on the starboard side

was served by a crew of six. At the gunner's commands, the barrel was unplugged and loaded with powder and shot, then Canfield and the others leaned on the tackle and waited the word to run out the gun. Since running out would be considered a hostile act by the English ship, that order would not be given unless hostilities were unavoidable.

Canfield heard the gun captain muttering to himself, "Where's the priming powder?"

Fine grained, carefully dried to be quick and dependable to flash, priming powder was used in the touchhole to ignite the bigger charge that propelled the shell. But there was no priming powder onboard; *Chesapeake* had mistakenly sailed without it.

Just as this calamity was discovered, a pair of shots boomed from the *Leopard*, bracketing the American ship with splashes. Then before any other orders could be given, the dreadful rolling thunder of a broadside shattered the day.

Forward of Canfield's position, a shell smashed through the unopened port of gun number one. The explosion lifted the cannon off its carriage, crushing two men. Splinters ripped from the hull, killing a sailor on the opposite side of the deck. A rending crash overhead told the story of shattered rigging, accompanied by the dreadful wails of more wounded men.

"Run out! Run out!" was the frantic cry.

Heaving at the tackle, number three was run out and trained on the enemy. With more shots tearing into their side, *Chesapeake*'s crew tried to fight back. Canfield dribbled coarse powder into the touchhole while the gun captain swung the slow match to keep it sizzling. The crew jumped aside from the recoil as the gunner touched the match to the powder, which fizzed and . . . did nothing. "Fouled!" the gunner cried. "Clear it! Clear it!"

Canfield snatched a rigging knife from his trousers and dug at the touchhole with its spike, even as another broadside hammered against the *Chesapeake*'s hull.

"Fire! Fire! In the name of heaven, why don't you fire?"

The limping, bandaged, and outraged crewmen of *Chesapeake* were mustered on deck under the watchful eye of the same disdainful British lieutenant. Accompanied this time by a contingent of Royal Marines bearing muskets, he ranged up and down the rows of sailors. "You," he said, indicating a brawny bosun's mate. "You are a deserter."

"I'm not! Born in New York."

The British officer ignored the pleas. "Deserters can be shot. Go into the launch." Then the lieutenant stopped in front of Canfield. "What are you rated?"

"Carpenter's mate," Canfield replied. "Born slave but now a freeman of Balt'Mer City." His frame, sturdy and springy as birch, tensed from neck to narrow waist as he waited what followed.

The Englishman had selective eyes and ears. "Carpenter, eh? We need one of those. Deserter, go into the launch."

Commodore Barron sputtered, "Do you not even make a pretense of it? That man is no more British than Napoleon!"

"We do not make pretenses," was the sneering reply. "We make examples."

"I'll not go back to bein' a slave," Canfield said. "Not for nobody."

"Five days bread and water and four-dozen lashes will change your mind," the lieutenant commented.

CHAPTER 1

———— ❦ ————

Fingering a silver spoon, dark-haired, thirty-two-year-old William Sutton watched fragrant steam waft from a tureen of turtle soup. It was, he reflected, too heavy and hot a concoction for this warmish, late May evening. The fashion-conscious Americans of 1812, driven by their envy of European society, always insisted on style at the expense of comfort. The crock's cover had been lifted with a flourish by an elderly Negro servant wearing white gloves and tailcoat, who then proceeded to ladle out the course to the twenty occupants of the dining salon.

Resplendent with silks, brass fittings, and linen-fold paneling, the rectory of St. Paul's parish, Baltimore, was furnished as elegantly as the Sutton home back on the heights of Hampstead in London.

William vowed to have as much and even more again, provided no ill-advised war interfered.

The recollection of what had been lost made William's green eyes flash with anger. America was his home and had been these six years past, ever since he and his grandfather had been falsely accused of treason and the family forced to flee for their lives. But his anger was not directed at England. Rather, William's ire was reserved for those who would plunge the young American nation into a war. Such a conflict could not help but be destructive to everything William had achieved. Worse, one of the war hawks was Grandfather Sutton, whose spare, bony frame was seated two places to William's right, on the other side of William's honey-blond sister-in-law, Angelique.

When three courses for which William had little appetite had been presented and removed, Grandfather Sutton engaged in spirited conversation with the thin-lipped man with the bulging eyes placed across from him: U.S. Secretary of State James Monroe. "Even if the present crisis can be settled," Grandfather insisted, "there is yet a need for a strong national defense, and that must begin with a substantial navy. Barbary pirates will prey upon our shipping even after Britain ceases to harass our sailors. Meaning no disrespect to our dining companion, of course."

The transparently insincere apology was offered to Lieutenant Benton Hazzard of His Britannic Majesty's frigate *Politic*, which was anchored in Baltimore Harbor. William had glimpsed the warship from the top of Chapel Hill before going into supper.

If William's grandsire was attempting to get a rise out of the British officer, he did not succeed. The blond-haired Hazzard lifted his glass politely and declared, "Respect is the beginning of understanding between individuals and nations alike."

William's twin, Albert Penfeld, had been raised as French after a shipwreck in infancy in which the boys' father had died. He was only reunited with his family a short while before they were turned out of England. Albert took up his grandfather's cause. "Surely the Orders in Council by which Britain demands a tax from those who would trade in Europe, and the forcible impressing of American sailors onto British ships, are issues clearly comprehended and offensive."

As the acting head of the American Coastal Shipping Company, the Sutton family shipping firm, William understood the grievances that had brought the United States and Britain to the brink of war, and yet it was his position that no matter how many men were lost to press-gangs, the inconvenience was slight compared to how trade would suffer if war erupted. "I have no reason to speak well of British policy, but England has been fighting against Bonaparte for a decade. The French emperor is just as repressive regarding trade. It is our duty . . . our duty . . . ," he repeated, forcefully underscoring the point, "to remain neutral until the European conflict is resolved. Only by keeping out of war can our nation continue to prosper and grow."

Her heart-shaped face looking concerned, Dora, William's wife, seated beside attorney Francis Scott Key, spoke up in the diffident tone that had, over the past year, so perversely irritated William. "Surely it must be terrifying for passengers on a peaceful merchant vessel to be stopped at sea by a warship bristling with cannons. I know I . . ." At a glimpse of the harshness printed on William's face Dora halted. "That is, whose ever cannons they were."

"It is never our intent to afright the ladies, mum," Lieutenant Hazzard maintained. "But it is our lawful duty to recover deserters. Even sentence them to hang, if they resist, like Hercules Shraider."

The Reverend John Gruber, pastor of the Light Street Methodist Church, disagreed. "Deserters, hey? What about Amos Franklin of this city? American-born and yet forcibly removed from the ship *Lodestar* and made to serve for three years on a British warship, in engagements wherein he might have been killed, until he escaped in Brazil and made his way home. What about him?"

"And all the rest," Grandfather Sutton growled. "Albert, how many sailors have we lost to the press?"

"Twenty-five," was Albert's prompt reply. "Enough in the last five years to crew a schooner."

Angered his grandfather had called upon his brother for information about the family business rather than on him, William shot back, "In fairness, five of those men *were* actual British deserters. As for the others . . ."

"Unfortunate mistakes," Hazzard commented smoothly.

"It must feel like more than an unfortunate mistake to be carried off against your will for three years of your life," Dora said indignantly. "Imagine not being able to go home. What if loved ones at home died during the absence? What if Mister Franklin had died in a battle, and his family never knew his fate?"

"Dora," William said with a tone of warning,

"neutrality is the policy of the American Coastal Shipping Company and of this nation. Am I right, Mister Secretary? We must maintain strict neutrality or risk much worse than one man's unplanned voyage."

"Not worse to the one who was taken," Dora observed. "What if it were you? And if the English navy kidnaps our men, have they not already violated our neutrality?"

"Enough!" William blurted, his hand slap on the table making the crystal glasses dance and spilling his wine. "Neutrality," he said again through gritted teeth. "You'll have to pardon my wife, Lieutenant. She speaks out of emotion and not knowledge, and moreover has not been feeling well recently. You may be excused, my dear."

"Yes, William," Dora said softly with downcast eyes.

"I will accompany her," Albert's wife, Angelique declared. The gleam in her gray eyes belying her calm words. "We ladies leave the field of battle to you, gentlemen."

Silenced by the disapproval of her husband, Dora climbed into the carriage beside Angelique.

Hot tears of humiliation burned her eyes as William barked orders to the driver, and the whip snapped onto the backs of the team. Only when the coach lurched forward did Dora cast a sideways glance out the window at the glowing lights of St. Paul's rectory, and at William striding back into the house.

Angelique sighed as they passed the two imposing structures of the Anglican church of St. Paul's and the Roman Catholic cathedral of St. Peter's. Each building rivaled the other for size, beauty, and position on the steep slope known as Chapel Hill, which overlooked the crowded waterside docks of Baltimore.

"It is hard sometimes to believe William and Albert are brothers, is it not?" Angelique commented, trying to lighten Dora's palpable misery. "Though they look much alike on the outside, like your St. Paul and my St. Peter, they go to war with one another over matters I cannot comprehend."

Dora replied with a nod. She was grateful when the brightness of the oil lamps receded, and the interior of the coach concealed her wounded expression. Angelique reached out and grasped Dora's hand in sympathy.

"I should not have interrupted," Dora said.

"I am glad you did, *cherie*. *Oui!* Else the two of us would still be sitting there among the war council staring down upon the pudding and longing to be home to remove our corsets and kiss our children good night!" She laughed.

Dora smiled for the first time since the ordeal had begun. "It was rather like a summons to court, wasn't it?" She recalled how excited she had been at the prospect of supper among the leading citizens of Baltimore. How she and Angelique had chosen silk fabrics from bolts at the Sutton warehouse and each had evening dresses sewn from the latest European designs.

"*Oui!*" Angelique tugged at the waist of her gown. "Too tight! Unlike the men I gave no thought of expanding my empire at such a meal. Three bites of the English roasted beef, and I could no longer breathe. And then such talk! *Mon Dieu!* They expect us to swallow politics that would choke a horse!"

How grateful Dora was for Angelique. Though Dora was as English as roast beef, and Angelique as French as paté, they had grown ever closer since they had come to America together with their husbands. They had lived together in a small town house for the first eighteen months in Baltimore.

After her first son, Cyrus, Angelique had given birth to a second baby boy, Paul. At the same time Dora lost a baby girl at birth. A deep friendship had been forged in the fires of adversity during those difficult days, but as the Sutton shipping firm was slowly being rebuilt after its glorious days in England and the subsequent and necessary move to America, the brothers grew further apart.

At first Angelique had spoken only a smattering of broken English. But she learned quickly from the cheerful Scottish housekeeper, Mrs. Honeywell, as well as from the common fishmongers and vegetable sellers in Baltimore's market square. Unlike Dora, who had left the familiarity of England and become more timid and cautious in her new country, Angelique's adopted language was unfettered, spiced with honesty and humor. "My mouth," she was fond of saying, "wears no corset."

Her husband, Albert, adored her. Only last year she had presented him with Jeannine, a baby girl who was the image of herself. Albert had been known to dance around the parlor after 2:00 A.M. feedings, singing songs about his two angels.

Last autumn, when Dora had miscarried a second child near full term, William had become more distant and preoccupied with his work. Dora was a loving mother to William's six-year-old son, Billy, even though he was the product of William's wild youth. She longed to give William children from her own body!

"It will be, *cherie!*" Angelique encouraged. "I shall ask the Virgin to pray for you! You will see!"

Unfortunately, it would take a miracle like the Virgin Mary experienced for Dora to conceive. William rarely shared Dora's bed these days. This was one fact Dora had not confided in Angelique. The pain of William's rejection was too great. Questions plagued her. Was it another woman? Or was he truly married to his work as he often claimed? The warmth of their first love had cooled and congealed until nothing flowed between them. Her longing for his attention irritated him; his disdain made her childlike and uncertain where she had once been strong and confident.

In spite of this, Dora did not envy Angelique, but rather admired her. Angelique was a Catholic, Dora the daughter of an Anglican minister, and yet the two women prayed for one another to the one Savior. Angelique was gray-eyed, blond-haired, and in the vibrancy of rounded womanhood, strong and healthy. Dora, blond but dark-eyed, was fragile. One French. The other English. Were two personalities ever so opposite? And yet the kinship of womanhood broke through every barrier.

As though Angelique read her thoughts she remarked, "We have no wars between us women and look! Men! They should take the lesson from us, should they not? Then there would be no talks of war, eh? Foolish men. I will give Albert the piece of my brain when he gets home tonight. Tonight he can sleep with Pauly and Cyrus! *Mon Dieu!* Between the two boys he can sleep! A foot in the face! A fist in the ear! How do they sleep? Napoleon and Wellington at war! A night between them, and Albert will not think of fighting English ships!"

"You wouldn't do that to him," Dora said with a chuckle at the image.

"Would I not? How else would he be reminded of the best things in life? A good night's sleep. An attentive woman to wake up to. What else will keep a man from going to war or . . ." Angelique paused to compose a suitable parallel. "Or chasing after a foreign sail? *Oui.* I know how to keep Albert in his place. One way or the other I see he is too tired to fight or to wander far."

The humor of the comments fell flat as Dora was reminded of her own failure. William fought his battles silently, and as to his wandering . . . "I wish William would look at me with the same love Albert looks at you," Dora blurted.

Angelique softened. "Ah, *cherie,* I did not mean . . ."

"No. It's true. William is not . . . I don't believe he loves anything more than American Coastal Shipping Company." Her words stopped far short of her fears.

"It is an English habit, this preoccupation with commerce, is it not? William loved you first, *cherie.* Who would not? So sweet with your heart-shaped face! Much sweeter than I am, to be sure. But these Englishmen. Work! Work! Work! The ships! Business! I see this clearly when we first came to this country and lived in our little house. Tell the truth, I would have to kill your William if he was Albert, and I was married to him. Though they appear alike I can tell them apart instantly by the thoughts in their eyes."

"I think it is because William has just me to look at."

"No! No! No! In France you would have men lined up to kiss your shadow! No! It is a way of living, I think! Too bad both brothers were not washed onto the soil of France to start. In France a woman can say to her man, 'Get out of bed and go to work!' And the husband says, 'I have more important work to do for France right where I am!'" Angelique crossed herself and whispered confidentially, "I swear to you that is the true nature of a Frenchman. This is why I have long suspected Napoleon is the devil! He has cast a spell upon the men of France. How else could Napoleon keep so many Frenchman away from the single work they truly love—the populating of France?"

Again Angelique made Dora laugh in spite of her grim thoughts. "You shouldn't say such things in polite society, you know."

"*Oui.* Not polite society. But to you! And I'll tell you more! These men do not admit it, but I know it is so. This is the reason the French will one day give up these grand dreams of empire! *Oui!* They'll dream the same dream one night, get up from their army camp, go home to bed, and there will be peace once again in the world!"

A single oil lamp illuminated the hallway as Dora entered the house. The housekeeper, Mrs.

Honeywell, had gone to bed long ago. Young Billy was sleeping over at Angelique and Albert's home tonight, no doubt enjoying the lively company of his cousins.

Dora stood listening to the ticktock of the tall clock William had had specially crafted for her by old Mr. Pelsner, the Fell's Point clock maker. William had presented it to her on their fifth wedding anniversary with the words, "So you will remember I love you for all time."

The sweetness of his sentiment had grown bitter over the last year. The chimes of the timepiece served to remind her of the hours William spent away from her in the offices of American Coastal Shipping or weeks and months away at sea. Soon he and Albert would be leaving again. Although Albert always sailed away from Baltimore reluctantly, William acted eager to go. What had she done to drive William from her? Was his aloofness from her merely his way of coping with the loss of two children, as Angelique had once said?

Dora made her way up the steep stairs to her bedroom. Blowing out the lamp, she undressed in the dark, donned her white cotton nightgown, and sat beside the open window to wait for William.

Waiting for William had become a ritual. From the hall, the chimes marked ten o'clock.

A slice of golden light widened in the doorway of the rectory of the Episcopal church. Two sets of silver-buckled boots emerged, heel tacks clicking on the stoop. By the third step down, formal black waistcoats enclosing nearly identical forms emerged as William and Albert turned right on Cathedral Hill road.

The night smelled of rye bread baking, of peppered meat with red sauce, and humid, early summer. William breathed in air so thick it was like warm oatmeal in his lungs. The twin brothers strolled at an easy pace, but a perceptible tension prolonged their silence almost a block before either said a word.

It was the English way, William considered, to be private; reticent to share. Even brothers had to ponder at length before they could admit to their own thoughts. Finally William broke the quiet. "England seems far away after six years."

Albert eyed him sideways. "And France equally distant, if not more. I used to think in French and then translate for myself, but anymore I think in English . . . no matter. We are as American as any men can be. And we have our business, our lives, our *families* here in America."

"Families . . . ," William grumbled as he was reminded of Dora. "It is as if she doesn't know when to keep her mouth shut! To think we were sitting with Hazzard, a man who, in another setting, could have me arrested for treason. Dora shamed me by her persistent stubbornness!"

Albert, formulating a cautious reply, did not speak right away. "Could she be right, though? It was a good point she made. What if it *was* you taken? Or what if it was me? Would my wife and children not be heartbroken?"

"And children," said William, scowling, avoiding the point entirely. "Dora hasn't been the same since the failure of her second pregnancy. She has been clingy and needy, and when she's not she goes deliberately in the opposite way. It's as if I can never win."

William tromped on, Albert followed, gazing up at the infinite number of summer stars, blazing with cool fire above the torpid Baltimore air.

Turning his view down the hill, William looked over the slumbering brick buildings, still radiating heat into the night. Yet in hours those same structures would be scrambling and swarming with packing, loading, hauling, leaving . . .

"Leaving," he snapped, addressing Albert, who could not be distracted from his view of the heavens.

The idea of a departure made William happy. "Just think, Albert. In hours we will be aboard the *Julia,* on the high seas, bound for the premier tobacco and cotton port of South Carolina. I sense it: we are about to grab the tail of a comet as far as our fortunes are concerned."

Albert squinted toward the port, skeptically examining it. "I prefer a portent more reliable than a comet," he said. "My blazing star is my home, and my fortune is my wife and children."

Was Albert merely confused, or possibly unaware of what riches lay in waiting for a man who would seize the opportunity, William wondered. "But I mean our *fortunes* . . . riches and prestige like you never dreamed of, if we work for it," William said, desperate to make his brother understand. "We must rebuild the Sutton shipping empire beyond what it once was in Britain."

"But why is that necessary? Why must we be the biggest?"

"Because in America, no one can stop us, and

we can leave our mark!" William responded with arms outstretched and hands reaching to grasp the future. "It's a new life, a new world, and the rewards are for the taking. The more one hazards, the more one stands to gain. The more freedom one has to succeed, the more expansive the success can be. Fortune favors the bold, eh?"

"William," Albert said patiently, "life is a chance for freedom and success and some of those things. The rewards of hard work allow us to have less concern for the smaller details. The search for wealth is a grand and exciting adventure with much to be gained, to be sure, though there is always much to be lost . . . and the dangers are not merely financial."

"A trade-off," William replied. "Like deciding to invest in tobacco or cotton when there is only so much room on the ship and one has to choose."

"Exactly, William."

"But why not build a bigger ship? Then there is plenty of room for all."

"Are we speaking of cotton and tobacco or of life and family?" Albert prodded.

"Can't one have both?"

Albert shook his head. "To have wealth allows a kind of freedom, a freedom to sail and haul whatever you want. But if that is your singular focus, eventually you become enslaved by the thing that once made you free. A man's life can become a ship so cumbersome and costly that it is unmanageable. Then he is left to drift on his vast ship. And what mark or legacy is left behind when the one who left it is gone, drifted away?"

William frowned. "There is always someone to run the ship. There is always someone who will run it when he is gone. That will be a proper legacy."

"Maybe you're right," Albert conceded, tiring of the discussion. In French he said, "A different taste for every mouth."

William felt as though he had won the discussion. Maybe Albert was not yet convinced, but after the voyage William was certain he would be. "Shall we walk to the harbor and see the *Julia*?"

Closing tired eyes, Albert replied he would not. "We'll be there soon enough tomorrow and long enough onboard. For now I wish to see Angelique and my children."

Searching for reasons to postpone going home and making up with Dora, William replied, "I must go down and check that the food supplies have been properly stowed."

"You oversaw them yourself yesterday."

"But I should check that the papers are in order, review the logs . . ."

Albert stopped in front of his house. "You have done that also."

William looked anxiously around and down the street several doors to his own. "I'm sure there are details remaining that I should attend to tonight."

"Yes," said his twin. "For tonight, William, go home and be loving with your wife. The fortunes of tomorrow will come soon enough. The comet's tail will wait that long."

Concluding Albert was right, the brothers parted. Each set of clicking heels traced twin but vastly different lives up their own stoops.

It was past midnight when Dora heard the footsteps and Albert's and William's voices in the deserted street. Whatever dispute the brothers may have had over politics had vanished. William spoke in a sad voice. Did she hear him mention her name? Albert's tone was calm and sympathetic as they bade one another good night.

It was good, Dora thought, that William had Albert to confide in. But how she wished William would share his heart with her as he had when they first married.

The key turned in the lock. The door opened and closed quietly. There was a slight hesitation as William got his bearings in the featureless hallway, then carefully made his way up the stairs.

Since her last pregnancy he had slept in a separate bedroom, so she called to him as he passed her door.

"Are you awake?" he replied, contrite.

"Yes." She fought to control her trembling voice. "I . . . I'm sorry. I . . . shouldn't have . . ."

"No. No. I was too harsh with you."

Silence. The clock chimed the half-hour.

"William?"

He lingered in the corridor. She could smell tobacco on his clothes.

"What . . . Dora?"

"Would you sit with me awhile?"

In reply, he entered the pitch black of the room, bumped against the dresser, and sat down on the still-made bed.

"You've been sitting up?"

"I couldn't sleep."

"It's late. Albert and I were just . . . talking."

"All is well between the two of you?"

"He's my brother. He's also a Frenchman at heart with an intense loathing of what the English hold dear. But he is my brother."

"You've worked out your differences?" How she longed for William to work out whatever differences he had with her too.

"Never. We may be the mirror image of one another on the outside, but he has no practical head for commerce or . . . important matters of . . . Are you all right?"

"I miss you."

"Miss me?" He repeated the comment with a hint of irritation.

"I mean, I'll miss you . . . when you are sailing the *Julia*. Off with your true love."

"The sea is my mistress. You knew that when we married."

"I didn't mean to accuse. You act eager to be off. That's what I meant."

"The maiden voyage of the *Julia*. How could I not be eager?"

She sighed and stood, facing the sound of his voice. "I . . . yes . . . of course. You've lived for that ship. It's right you would want to sail her! It's . . . oh William! But it's right that I'll miss you. Want you!" She sat down on the opposite side of the bed and reached toward him. "I've been waiting up because . . ."

Taking his hand in hers, she held his fingers to her lips and then kissed his palm. His touch was reluctant at first and then, as if he resigned himself to the inevitable good-bye scene, he touched her cheek and drew her close to him. She began to cry.

"I'll be back soon enough," he soothed. His embrace was without passion. He held her as he would have held a child.

Kissing his chin, his face, his mouth, she whispered, "I need you . . . William . . . to love me."

Returning her kisses, he yielded to her desire, but she knew his thoughts were far away from her bed tonight.

CHAPTER 2

A forest of masts rose over Fell's Point where two ships of the American Coastal Shipping Company were being provisioned. Although Baltimore Harbor was plainly visible from the front steps of Dora and William Sutton's town house, the stench and bustle of the port were a world away. The air reeked with the smells of pitch and tar. Boarding-houses for thousands of sailors were wedged between the workshops of ship joiners, shipwrights, the forges of smiths, bustling chandleries, grog shops, and bordellos. It was here that vessels landed their cargoes and reprovisioned; here slaves were bought and sold on an open auction block. It was also here that the superbly fast sailing ships known as Baltimore clippers were built and launched.

The new flagship of the Sutton shipping enterprise was a Baltimore clipper. Three-masted and capable of carrying an immense press of canvas above her sleek hull, she was named *Julia* for the mother of William and Albert who had died shortly after their arrival in America. The tribute seemed fitting to the brothers, who considered the shining Baltimore clipper to be the mothership of their future hopes.

As the carriage rattled through the packed streets toward the quay, William pointed out the sharply raked masts of the *Julia* to young Billy.

"Can't I go with you and Uncle Albert, Father?" the child pleaded with Atlantic-blue eyes.

"Not this time," William said as he ruffled the boy's red hair.

Dora added, "There are warships on the prowl. Not a good time for lads to go a'sailing with their fathers."

"I can fight them," Billy declared, lowering an imaginary cannon and firing.

William laughed. "You're a fearsome opponent, but there'll be no duel at sea for us. And someday soon, if everything goes as I have planned, we'll have a whole fleet of ships like *Julia*."

"And will I then go sailing with you?"

"Better yet . . . I promise you'll be master of one of them."

William grinned at Dora as she raised an eyebrow at the wonder in the child's eyes. The gaze of the six-year-old was transfixed by the spanking-clean rigging and furled canvas of the sails as he dreamed of being the captain of his own vessel.

"He is so like you, William," Dora remarked.

William replied, "I remember my own dreams as I rode with Grandfather Sutton to the shipyards on the Thames. And again in the Royal Marines. Now here we are on Thames Street, a block away from Shakespeare Lane, but half a world away from London. I tell you, Dora, our American hearts have ties to England that will prevent war with our old comrades."

"You're thinking of your friend Thomas Burton?" she queried.

He nodded. "We fought Napoleon together as lowly marines." William's eyes clouded in thought. "It was good to hear he is alive and free in spite of how I saw his ship being attacked. Six years later he is still fighting the French, no doubt. But in Spain, in the Mediterranean, or . . . who can say where? I wouldn't like to give him reason to fight my adopted homeland. To meet me in battle, not as a friend but as a foe, especially since he has answered none of my letters since his escape from the French."

Dora clasped his hand. "So that is why . . ."

He turned away from her searching eyes, as if he did not want her to see his innermost thoughts. "I am content to be a merchant, more than content. It is all I want for myself and for my son. Albert would not mind a war, spouting as he does high-flown phrases about honor and respect of nations. As for me, there is more than blood that ties me to my native land."

"I dream of England sometimes. You miss it too?"

"I long to see London again one day. The dome of St. Paul's and, yes, even a glimpse of Hampstead Heath. But as an American merchant. A view from the Pool of London onboard my Baltimore clipper."

"Then will you take Billy and me with you?"

He smiled faintly. "We share that, do we? Both homesick?"

"Tell me one day you'll take me home to England, just for a short while. Then I'll lay flowers at my father's grave and see where Mother is buried. Show Billy where we first met and . . ."

Memories of those first days in love were too much for William. He whipped his head up and broke in. "And if all goes as planned with Gerald Fussel's scheme, our expanded fleet of clippers will become a reality sooner."

"Be wary of Mister Fussel," Dora urged, referring to the man who oversaw the interests of American Coastal Shipping in South Carolina. "I do not trust him."

Annoyed by what he saw as another emotional outburst with no substance behind it, William ignored Dora and addressed his son. "Look there, Billy. There is our schooner, *Heart of Allegiance*. See her there?"

The boy nodded vigorously. "She's not nearly as clean or new as *Julia,* is she, Father?"

"No, but she's got a brave and true heart. Takes to the sea like a duck to water. I sailed her with ease through a West Indies gale last October when seven other ships were sunk."

"She's more my size," Billy suggested.

"Then *Allegiance* will be yours one day." He shot a glance at the sun. "We're late. Albert no doubt is already aboard. Tide'll be turning in an hour." Tapping the roof of the carriage with his walking stick, he shouted for the coachman to hurry.

Dora was inexplicably hurt by William's impatience to be off. Knowing they would not see one another again for nearly three months, she wished he would show some sign of regret at their parting. She told herself it was the tide that hurried him, not that he was anxious to be away from her. But as the coach rolled onto the quay, she could not shake the sense he *wanted* to leave her, that perhaps she would never see him again.

"Ah, there! Albert's carriage! Angelique and the children have said their farewells."

Albert, a heartbroken expression on his face, stood upon *Julia*'s deck as Angelique herded the three children down the gangplank toward their coach. Tears streaked her pretty face.

William scoffed. "That lady was not meant to marry a sailor. All that blubbering, and Albert will only be gone to Charleston, then back to Baltimore on the *Allegiance* with a hold of tobacco. Not like my brave Dora, eh? Three months and . . ." He snapped his fingers, gave her a quick kiss, and leaped from the coach before it had stopped. Turning, he commanded cheerfully, "Don't get out. The quay is filthy."

"But . . . but . . . William! May we not board the *Julia*? See you to your quarters?" Dora protested.

"No time!" He was so happy. Embracing Billy through the open door, he blew her a kiss, promised to see her in three months, and shouted up to Albert, "Sorry I'm late!"

Albert, miserable to be sailing at all, gave a sheepish wave and returned his attention to his family's departure.

Clutching his belongings, William strode onto the ship without a look back. He did not see the tears that streamed down Dora's cheeks.

"What is it, Mother?" Billy asked her. "Why are you crying?"

"It's the smell of pitch in the air. Stings my eyes," she lied, not willing to let the boy know that perhaps she was not meant to be the wife of a sailor either.

A day and a half out of Baltimore and coming onto sunset at last, *Julia* and *Heart of Allegiance* traveled in easy comradeship. The schooner could sail nearer the eye of the wind than the square-rigged *Julia,* but with a fair breeze coming out of the northeast and astern, the *Julia* needed merely to reef main and topsails for the two ships to keep in company.

Although Albert would be returning to Baltimore in *Allegiance* with the cargo of tobacco, while en route to Charleston, he and William shared a cabin on the newer ship.

"Whist after supper?" William asked Albert as they stood at the rail. "Captain Drake and Doctor Sommers are agreeable."

Albert shrugged. "The mathematical counting of cards is so businesslike, it is more your game than mine, William. Me, I prefer dice and the fall of chance."

The sunset deepened from orange to a fiery red while the two men talked. *Allegiance*'s bow parted the placid waters some half-mile astern. Above the gull wing sails of the schooner, two fleets of clouds streamed toward the westering sun like the converging battle lines of warships. "Fair weather as far as Charleston," William predicted, quoting the adage about red skies at night. "An easy, uneventful, profitable trip."

The words had just left his lips when another sail was reported broad on the larboard beam. William went to the weather rail and lifted a brass telescope to his eye. "Frigate, by the look of her," he observed. "But ours or British I can't say."

"Should we try to go faster . . . just in case?" Albert asked.

Laughing and swallowing an arrogant reply made William turn as crimson as the sunset. Finally he gave up trying to stay polite and said, "Albert, sometimes I despair of making a seaman out of you. Look, if we crowd on more sail with the wind coming from so far astern we will run off and leave *Allegiance*. Besides that, the approaching vessel is to windward of us, meaning unless we give up our heading and run before the breeze altogether, she will still overtake us . . . perhaps have the legs of us even if we did. No," he concluded in a loud-enough voice to carry to Captain Drake, "we'll continue on course."

Within minutes it was apparent the new arrival intended to intercept the two cargo ships. As the courses converged, the lower sails, hull, and then the colors streaming from the masthead became apparent. "British frigate," William noted. "Could it be the *Politic* and our friend Hazzard?"

It could indeed.

A signal gun boomed, and the flags that broke out onboard the British warship called for the two Sutton vessels to heave-to. "Is it not time to run?"

Albert inquired. "We cannot allow members of our crew to be taken."

"Nonsense," William returned. "How can you even think such a thing after meeting Lieutenant Hazzard? This is nothing more than a chance meeting and a friendly greeting."

But Hazzard's manner was anything but friendly when he boarded the *Julia*, accompanied by a double file of armed marines. "Well, Misters Sutton," Hazzard said, "we meet again, although sooner than I expected. I'll have your log and manifest and your crew mustered on deck. Oh, and order your schooner to prepare for the same."

"You are not serious," William snorted. "You heard over our shared dinner that we are outbound for a cargo of cotton and tobacco . . . no contraband in those. And you concurred that unwarranted searches were unfortunate mistakes."

"Sutton," Hazzard replied brusquely, "you are wasting my time. I have my orders, so do you."

Being spoken to in such a manner onboard his pride and joy was more than William's carefully controlled temper could take. He lunged at the officer, but got no nearer than three feet before a pair of bayonet tips pressed into his waistcoat and halted his advance.

"This is an outrage!" William stormed, in concert with the stiffer breeze that hummed in the rigging. "I will . . ."

"Be careful what you threaten," Hazzard warned. "Now assemble the crew."

"Let me signal the *Allegiance* first," William said through gritted teeth. "So there is no misunderstanding."

In the failing light the signal lanterns William caused to be run up were acknowledged by a single beacon that bobbed in the wind from *Allegiance*'s foremast. Hazzard was smugly watching *Julia*'s crew lining up on her deck when his captain of marines shouted a warning and gestured toward the schooner. "She's making sail!"

William's message, delivered in private code to the captain of the smaller ship, had produced the intended result: *Allegiance* put her helm over, main, top, and jib sails were sheeted home, and the schooner bore up into the wind, crossing behind *Politic*'s stern.

Hazzard leaped toward the rail, waving his arms toward the observers on the British frigate. "Blast you, Sutton!" he yelled. "She'll stop if I have to sink her!"

William's temper exploded. He grabbed Hazzard

from behind in a wrestling hold, then spun round to face the astonished marines with the struggling lieutenant as a shield. "Go ahead and shoot!" he challenged. Despite Hazzard's screaming, the marines hesitated.

To Captain Drake, William shouted, "All sail. Let her run before the wind." And to the captain of the marines: "Drop your weapons, or I'll break his neck!"

Unused to being challenged or in any way thwarted in their high-handed searches, the British stood transfixed as Albert and Dr. Sommers relieved them of their weapons.

From the *Politic* a single cannon roared, and a ball raised a geyser of spray ahead of *Julia*'s prow. "Keep going!" William commanded. "They won't fire for effect if it endangers their own men."

Another shot landed astern, throwing up spray that the howling blow carried over the deck. "They have us bracketed, William," Albert cautioned.

"Keep going!" William said again. "They don't dare fire on us."

Running downwind, the distance between *Julia* and the British ship increased rapidly. The *Politic* had only a second to choose between unleashing a broadside or turning to pursue.

Another cannonball whistled overhead and punched a hole in the main topsail, then the bow of the pursuer swung round and the chase began.

"Dump these intruders into their launch," William ordered. "But knock a hole in it first."

Despite Hazzard's cursing and sputtering, the order was gleefully carried out and the foundering British rowboat soon dropped astern.

"They'll have to stop to retrieve them," William said with a hearty laugh. "Meanwhile we'll be away in the night and safe."

"But what about next time?" Albert argued. "Does this not mean war?"

"Next time we won't stop," William countered. "They won't fire on a neutral ship. If we don't heave-to, there will never be a next time."

Off the coast of South Carolina, where the Ashley and Cooper Rivers come together to form Charleston Harbor, William and Albert dropped anchor on the first of June. Four longboats rowed by dozens of shirtless, solidly muscled black men hooked on and towed the *Julia* to the docks. As far as the eye could see pyramids of cotton bales spanned the planks, while several hundred Negroes loaded and unloaded, stacked and unstacked, moving carts and wagons.

William trotted down the gangway with logbook and manifest in hand. The sweltering, honey-thick heat of the South poured over him. Albert followed, both men wobbling from the sea-sway that was no longer there.

"William, my boy!" shouted a big man with a ponderously meaty paunch that appeared to remain suspended only by the extremity to which his shoulders were thrown back.

"Gerald Fussel!" William retorted in the same booming way.

Fussel slapped William on the back harder than necessary. It made him jump and wince, and ruined his readjustment to having earth underfoot.

"Lost your land legs I see," Fussel guffawed, looking at Albert. "And I see you've brought the little brother along." Fussel, Northern by birth, had adopted Southern dialect, but at times it sounded false, as if put on.

His smile forced as he stuck out his hand, Albert asked, "How are you, sir? I am here for the tobacco. I will return to Baltimore aboard the *Heart of Allegiance*. That is, if she makes it in."

"Why?" Fussel demanded, glaring around as if

seeking someone to blame for an unknown misfortune.

William explained about the encounter with the *Politic*, to which Fussel alternately made growling noises and sympathetic murmurs. "Those blasted English . . . meanin' no disrespect of course . . . and I'm sure you're right. When they find they can't bully us, they'll leave us alone."

"In any case," Albert suggested, "*Allegiance* has escaped, for there she comes." He pointed out to the channel where the schooner could be seen approaching port.

Gerald slapped Albert on the back. "That's splendid," he boomed. "Come along. We'll have a bite to eat while my Negroes begin loadin' your cotton. But first, I want to show you somethin'."

That the two brothers regarded Fussel in distinctly different ways was evident from their manner. William appeared to merge personalities with Gerald, the big-bellied, cigar-smoking merchant prince, while Albert remained distant, as though miles away.

Fussel led them up several flights of steps to a landing high above the docks. "Port Charleston," he announced proudly, scratching at a corner of his thick, graying mustache. "The biggest cotton and tobacco port on the coast of America and possibly the biggest anywhere."

William scanned the docklands as he listened, the commercially ambitious side of his nature swelling with the view.

"Ships in port from all over the world," Fussel boasted, as if he were personally responsible. "Just look at it. Thousands upon thousands of dollars changin' hands! Men like us gettin' rich while others do the work." He sighed in awe of his words. "This is grand enterprise, William."

Fussel grasped Albert by the forearm, insisting both brothers be overwhelmed with the grandeur of business. Albert shook loose from the grip, but Fussel did not notice.

The Sutton agent for the southern United States stuck out his finger, tracing the line of the wharves out to where distant shipmasts stood like toothpicks. Then, circling his finger and pointing to a much more confined area right in front of them, he said, "And this, this dock right here is yours."

Seeing the whole harbor, hundreds of ships, and miles of docklands contrasted with the minute portion labeled "Yours" made William feel inadequate and meager—and desperate to be recognized as a formidable shipper.

Smiling with tobacco-stained teeth, Fussel leaned in conspiratorially. "Doesn't it make you want to crack the whip and get goin' sooner?"

"Indeed," was William's restless reply.

With evident distaste Albert said, "You are using slaves now for your work, Mr. Fussel. It seems . . ."

Fussel cut him off. "You know me, 'Albear.'" Fussel made fun of the French pronunciation of Albert's name. "Everyone that likes me calls me Gerald. Anyway, in answer to your question, yes."

Albert wasted no time in expressing his feelings when he continued with his question. "Right. Mister Fussel, thinking back over the invoices you have forwarded to American Coastal Shipping, I recall seeing an extensive bill for labor recently."

Fussel strove to backtrack. "Of course a man has to charge for his labor, doesn't he? There are costs, like purchasin' slaves, feedin' them, and all those whips and chains we've got to buy." He laughed boisterously to show this last was meant as humor, taking William in again. Then he continued, "If you're tryin' to pin me as pocketin' a pretty penny for myself, then you're right. That's what sharp business is about. Right, William? Makin' as much money as possible while minimizin' expenses?" He bobbed forcefully to provide a show of support for his own words.

Though Albert narrowed his eyes, William's response mirrored Fussel's. "That's right! And the money in the middle is called profit."

"That's my boy!" Fussel applauded explosively with a swat that was hard enough to make William choke. "Yes, sir, and a lot of profit it is too. So much that I'm able to give a twenty percent discount on labor costs. Did you see that on the invoice?"

"I recall something of that nature," Albert admitted at last, feeling somehow out-foxed.

"I figured you would." Fussel eyed Albert, speaking bluntly in a bluff, no-nonsense tone meant to express sincerity. "Albert, politics aside, I want you to know I'm not unhappy anymore about losin' the Northern operation of Sutton to you. I think you're a great chap, and besides, I'm doin' better down here than I did when I was runnin' both halves from up north." He stuck out his hand to assure Albert there were no hard feelings.

William watched Albert consider the gesture. A lot of the proud Frenchman that remained in Albert would have to be taken out, William decided. This was America, and things were done differently.

As Albert took Fussel's hand solemnly, Fussel's booming merriment covered up the awkwardness.

Her hold loaded with bales of tobacco, *Heart of Allegiance* rode lower in the water, but still danced over the Atlantic like a stone skipping across a pond. When Albert commented on this glide to *Allegiance*'s captain, a Nantucketer by the name of Reed, he was informed his observation was correct but not original. It was from the Dutch word for skipping stones —*scoon*—that the craft took its name.

"Oh," Albert said, sensing that perhaps his brother was entirely right; Albert would never make a sailor. Then with characteristic self-assurance he got his mood back on an even keel by reminding himself he would be home again in two more days at most. His boys and his angels—Angelique of the honey-blond hair and the baby who looked so much like her—would be waiting. Albert's view of the golden strand of the shoreline and the snowy embrace of the ocean swell merged with his vision of his wife. How fortunate he was, Albert thought.

The two Sutton vessels had departed Charleston Harbor at the same time and had sailed in convoy for the first leg. The evening before, however, they had parted from each other. *Julia* had cruised farther offshore to pick up the westerlies that would carry her to Europe while *Allegiance* continued beating into the wind up the coast.

Allegiance was off Cape Hatteras when the helmsman, seventeen-year-old Stephen Birch, called Albert's attention to the sail bearing up on them from the southeast. "Not another British frigate," Albert remarked anxiously. "Fate could not be that unkind."

"I'm afraid so," Captain Reed responded, offering Albert the telescope. "The blockade is closer than ever. Here in sight of land they can't pretend to be on the high seas. What do you want me to do?"

Mindful of William's strict instructions and of his own inadequacy as a naval commander, Albert shrugged. "Sail on, of course. My brother informs me they will not actually fire to strike us."

Reed was doubtful. "That hole in *Julia*'s sail I saw being repaired at Charleston wasn't made by a flying fish."

"Nevertheless," Albert replied, "my brother assured me it was an accident. The British mean to harass and annoy and intimidate, but not to cause a serious incident with a neutral nation. They have their hands full with the emperor, William says, and this much I know to be fact."

When the British signal gun barked its order to heave-to, Captain Reed nodded to the helmsman to hold to his course, then suggested tactfully to Albert that the *Allegiance* edge closer toward shore. "Lots of sandbanks in these waters," he noted. "*Allegiance* draws a lot less water than that frigate. Maybe they won't try to follow."

Albert agreed, but the strategy apparently did not please the pursuers. The frigate fired a warning shot that imitated a skipping rock better than the schooner. The ball struck the water astern, bounded onward, hit the surface again at a low angle, and bounced upward to smack into the Sutton vessel's side.

"They mean business," Stephen Birch said. "What do we do?"

His apprehension growing, Albert remained mindful of William's position. "That was a warning shot and not intentional," he said. "Keep going!"

A pair of blasts erupted from the frigate's bow chasers. One of the balls passed harmlessly overhead, but the other crashed through *Allegiance*'s side at the waterline.

"That's no warning!" Reed urged. "Is a cargo of tobacco worth dying for?"

Gritting his teeth, Albert replied, "Can we outrun them?"

"Only if we get inside the banks where they can't follow," was the reply. "There's a narrow passage right ahead."

"Do it!"

More shots fountained water over the schooner; then another volley, and this time shells found their marks. One collided with the aft boom, shattering it and shredding the sail. The second clipped the rudder, spinning the wheel, throwing the helmsman to the deck, and making *Allegiance* yaw like a drunkard.

Reed and Albert grabbed for the tiller, but too late. The schooner plunged her bow onto the sandbank, heeling over sharply and tumbling the crew.

Another shot followed, hitting the identical spot as the earlier blow to the rigging aft and reducing the mast to a stump. "Strike the colors," Reed implored, "before they hammer us to kindling!"

Even as Albert agreed and Birch jumped up to haul down the flag, yet another shell impacted *Allegiance* on the railing.

Young Stephen Birch, on his first voyage away from his Baltimore home, was in the act of struggling with the hoist when the nine-pound cannonball hit. As the others were prostrate on the deck, he was the lone one injured. As if in slow motion, he fumbled with the line till the American flag floated loose and tumbled downward. Only then did he fall forward to land beside Albert. "Sorry I . . . couldn't . . . faster," he mumbled, and then he died.

Kneeling beside Birch's crumpled form at the foot of the fractured mast, Albert did not even get up when the marine guard attending Lieutenant Hazzard prodded his ribs with a bayonet. "You killed him," Albert said at last. "Why?"

"You cannot blame me," Hazzard replied, sniffing in unconcern. "You did not heave-to when ordered, nor did you yield when we fired a warning round. That you were fleeing is proven by the fact you have run aground. Consider yourself lucky."

"Lucky?" Albert mouthed bitterly. "Shall I tell that to the boy's parents?"

"If you had not struck your colors when you

did, your ship would have been battered to pieces as soon as our broadside was brought to bear. Stand when I speak to you."

Albert drew himself upright. "Have you not satisfied yourself about our cargo and crew? Tobacco, American grown like this child."

"Yes," Hazzard said absently. "A pity about the tobacco . . . ruined by the seawater I imagine. But enough of this: Where is your brother? Where is the *Julia*?"

Albert's steely eyes lifted from Birch's body and locked with the lieutenant's. "You cannot imagine I would answer you," he said.

"No," Hazzard admitted, "thought not. Well, he had better hope you see him before I do. I thought there was something familiar about the Sutton name, and now it has been confirmed; you are that notable family of traitors from six or eight years back."

Clenching and unclenching his fists, Albert said, "You would not dare say such things if you were not backed by muskets and cannons."

"No? Hear this then: If it comes to war, your brother and grandfather will be facing the gallows for aiding and abetting the enemy. And the single reason we won't hang *you* is your being French."

"I am every inch a Sutton," Albert said proudly. "Be warned, *monsieur*. We Suttons make true friends, but also every bit as faithful enemies."

Hazzard's staccato guffaw sounded more like a barking cough. "The leak is plugged, and the rising tide will float you free. At our next encounter you will acknowledge my commands more rapidly or suffer the consequences."

The *Allegiance* limped into port under the tug of the undamaged headsail alone. The tatters of her main and the stump of the mizzen telegraphed the disaster to the watchers on the hills around Chesapeake Bay faster than any signal flags. Though the cause was not known, so quickly did the identity of the battered ship reach Baltimore that Grandfather Sutton already waited on the dock.

Unable to maneuver, *Allegiance* anchored in the stream, and Albert was rowed ashore.

"Where is William?" was Grandfather's anguished query when he saw Albert alone.

Divining the fear behind the question, Albert answered promptly, "He's unhurt, Grandfather. He and the *Julia* are carrying on to Portugal."

"And this?" Grandfather said, indicating with

a lift of his bushy eyebrows the damaged schooner. "We've had no word of a squall."

The crew members who had rowed Albert ashore were surrounded by Baltimore citizens, as were the two Suttons, and excited talk swirled on the wharf. "There is no keeping it secret," Albert acknowledged. "Better the truth at once: we were accosted by a British frigate and fired on when we did not halt. That damage is the result, but there is more. Stephen Birch, Ordinary Seaman, was killed and buried at sea."

"So it will be war at last!" shouted someone in the crowd. "President Madison cannot hide his head in the sand after this!"

"It's the *Leopard* and the *Chesapeake* come again!" clamored another, "but no smoothing it over!"

Clutching his grandfather by the elbow, Albert said urgently, "Anger will ride down reason, but truly the government in Washington must be informed of what has happened."

"You and I will go together, my boy," Grandfather said. "We'll leave at once."

CHAPTER 3

———— ❧ ————

Dora and Angelique sat together, sewing, in the cool of the garden as Billy and Cyrus played with tin soldiers by the elm tree.

The first din of the mob gathered at the harbor reverberated like a distant cheering. The women glanced up curiously.

"Sounds like it's coming from the market."

Angelique closed one eye and held up her darning needle as a thought came to her. "Remember when the big swine broke free from his pen? And the tusks? And the snortings of him? All a'bristling he was. And he chased the slave auctioneers into the bay? What a jolly day that was."

"Too much to hope for a second time, I'm afraid." The roaring of the crowd increased.

"Maybe the old mad King George is dead then?"

"Reason enough for Baltimore to cheer." Dora laid down her fabric and hurried from the garden, through the house, and out onto the front stoop.

Angelique, asking Mrs. Honeywell to watch the children, hurried after her.

Shielding her eyes against the sun, Dora peered down the slope of the hill toward the harbor. There, amid the forest of masts, she spotted a crowd numbering in the thousands swarming over the quay near the American Coastal Shipping Company.

She gasped but did not have time to speak before the clatter of iron hooves against the cobbles and the shouting of a messenger hailed her.

"Madame Sutton! Madame Sutton!" It was young Dan Farmer, an accounting clerk from the shipping office.

"*Mon Dieu!*" Angelique cried. "What has happened!"

Dora was trembling as Farmer reined up and leaped from the saddle. Snatching off his cap, he looked fearfully from one woman to the next. "Madames Sutton," he began breathlessly, "something most terrible, I fear! Where to begin! Where, where, where!"

"*Oui!*" Angelique clutched Dora's arm. "At the beginning, idiot! Get on with it, scoundrel! Before we two die of frights!"

"The English fired upon *Heart of Allegiance*!" he blurted with her encouragement. "Cannonballs through the rigging! She's returned to harbor alone. When Mister Sutton saw her coming he sent me to fetch you."

"And the *Julia*?" Dora asked hoarsely.

"She didn't come back, ma'am."

"Sunk then?" The world spun around Dora.

"I'm sure I don't know," Farmer said, baffled.

"Don't know!" Angelique was outraged. "What have you come to tell us then?"

He began again patiently. "*Heart of Allegiance* is grievously damaged. A sailor shouted from the deck that it was the English who done it and that there was dead onboard. Then . . . away I rode."

"I'm feeling faint." Dora groped for the rail.

Angelique cowed Farmer with a withering look. "See what you've done! Half the news is no news!"

"But Mister Sutton sent me . . ."

"*Oui!* To get you out of the way, no doubt. And you will get out of *my* way or I shall . . . how do you say? . . . I shall kill the messenger?"

Farmer's eyes widened with terror. "Madame!"

"You do not even know if our husbands are dead and our children fatherless?"

"No, madame."

"Could they be . . ." Dora barely managed to speak.

Angelique held Dora's arm as her knees began to buckle. "Get in the house, dear Dora. It would not do for you to lie down splat upon the stoop before this ignorant yapping dog. He makes the noise but gives no information." Angelique gave Dora a guiding nudge toward the door, then snatched the reins from Farmer's hand, jumped onto the mounting block, and then onto the back of the nag.

Dora held onto the door latch in amazement as Angelique spun the horse on its heel and galloped back down the road. Billy and Cyrus crowded out the front to flank her.

"What is it, Mother?" Billy asked.

Dora did not, could not, reply, but fixed her gaze on the harbor.

"What is wrong, Mister Farmer?" Cyrus demanded.

Farmer raised his right hand solemnly. "I'm sure I don't know."

"Where's my mother gone off to?"

"She's taken my horse," Farmer replied.

"But where?" Cyrus continued to query.

Mrs. Honeywell, the babies on her hip, piped, "Hush, now. Hush, Cyrus. We'll know the straight of it soon enough."

Only moments passed before the tumult from the waterfront increased and began rolling over the rooftops toward Cathedral Hill.

After three minutes a coach appeared, surrounded by the mob. Billy leaped to his feet and cried, "There's your mother, Cyrus! Look there! She's riding beside Grandfather's carriage! And see there! Uncle Albert is beside Grandfather!"

But where was William? Dora struggled to her feet and staggered to the mounting block at the curbside. She climbed up, hoping for a better view. "William," she whispered.

Suddenly Angelique waved broadly to Dora. Urging the horse into a gallop she ascended the steep grade shouting, "They are well! William and Albert are unharmed! The *Julia* sails on! But the scurvy English will pay bloody dear if they ever come to Baltimore!"

Bumping over rutted clay roads, the Sutton carriage closed the forty-mile gap that separated

Baltimore from Washington in a plume of haze and choking grit. Plucking at the soggy folds of the stock that threatened to cut off his breath, Albert wondered again how Maryland summers could in the same month produce air so humid and lanes so dusty. Hard on the heels of that notion he mused at the location chosen for the American capital. Cold and foggy in winter, sweltering and mosquito-ridden in summer, the site had little to recommend it.

Grandfather Sutton, following Albert's gaze toward the pigsties and dairy sheds that adjoined two-story homes on the outskirts of the city, must have guessed Albert's speculation for he commented wryly, "Americans thrive on adversity, and sometimes they go out of their way to attain it."

Clumps of buildings dotted a landscape displaying more sheep than people, more cattle than commerce. "But the good citizens of Washington have their limits," Albert observed. "Perhaps they have left for the summer."

"Not all," Grandfather corrected. "Look there! Stop the carriage!"

The cause of this alarm was plain; the few people in sight were gathered in a crowd around a minuscule clapboard building bearing a sign: *The*

Federal Standard. As Albert and his grandfather watched, two men, their clothing shredded and their faces bloodied, escaped from the mob by crawling and then taking to their heels.

A third was not so lucky, being dragged down the wooden steps of the office with a noose around his neck. "Federalist Party newspaper," Grandfather noted. "Antiwar sentiment is not popular today. Looks like a lynching."

Albert was out of the carriage and running toward the scene before his grandsire could warn him against it. "You men," Albert called, his French accent returning thickly in his excitement. "Do not do this!"

"Keep back," a swarthy man in a blacksmith's apron growled. "Miller here has it comin'! Printin' words against teachin' them English a lesson." He raised his victim to the knees by yanking up on the corded rope. "But it's his turn in the woodshed now."

"Why do you do this? Can you not speak freely here, in this country? Napoleon kills those who disagree with him, but not here."

"Listen, crappaud," said the blacksmith coarsely. "Keep away from our business. The English has sunk ten of our ships and killed two hundred of our sailors! We would a been to war afore this except for the likes of this traitor."

So the news of the attack on the *Heart of Allegiance* had reached Washington, but in enormously garbled form. "But that is not the facts! I myself witnessed the attack by the English warship, and I am on my way to inform the president!"

The rest of the mob backed up a pace at this information, but the blacksmith was bulldog-like in his determination to carry out the intended hanging. "Maybe so and maybe we'll hang that worm Madison after we finish with Miller. Get out of the way!"

Albert, cool and diplomatic in the face of anger, was also smart enough to recognize when talk had failed. Without a thought for the number of angry faces in the crowd or the fact the blacksmith outweighed him by fifty pounds, he launched himself headlong, knocking the smith down.

The tumble allowed Editor Miller to escape lynching temporarily, but just far enough to loosen the knot around his neck and take a gasping breath.

The blacksmith, quick to recover, unleashed an overhand blow. Albert attempted to duck out of the way, but the press of the throng hemmed him in, and a fist the size of a top maul smacked into his ear, staggering him.

As the bigger man bored in, Albert lashed out with a flurry of lefts and rights of his own that drove the smith back. Like a maddened bull, Albert's assailant lowered his shoulders and prepared to charge again when a ragged volley of musketfire rang out over the heads of the mob.

Leading a handful of militiamen was Secretary of State Monroe. He and his troops were panting and out of breath, but the government official had the presence of mind to cover the fumbling soldiers by commanding, "Stop this civil disorder at once! If this street is not cleared in ten minutes, every man will be arrested for disturbing the peace!"

The mob outnumbered the militia ten to one, but Monroe's short speech had given the soldiers time to ready their muskets. There were grumbling and hostile commentary, but the crowd dispersed as ordered.

"Get up, Mister Miller," Monroe said, helping his political rival remove the noose. "I suggest you leave town for a few days. And you, Mister Sutton, seem to be at the center of every aspect of this crisis. Do you need a surgeon?" Monroe questioned.

Albert accepted a handkerchief from his grandfather and pressed it to the trickle of blood on his ear. Glancing down at his dirty and sweat-stained clothing, Albert said ruefully, "I am well enough to continue, unless you think my appearance too unsuitable."

"I think you look as serious as the matter at hand," Monroe replied. "The president is waiting."

Despite its squalid surroundings, the presidential mansion was a handsome enough home, not nearly as big or as interesting to look at as the forfeited Sutton estate in London, but presentable enough for a backwoods democracy. Liveried servants opened the carriage door and ushered Albert and his grandfather into the president's office.

President Madison rose from his Louis XIV rosewood desk. A diminutive man, dressed in black and wearing knee-length breeches that had last been fashionable at the turn of the century, Madison was unimpressive, to say the least. Albert was struck by how aptly Washington Irving had been in describing the chief executive as a "withered little applejohn."

Half a foot below Albert's stature, the president carried the gravity of his office with him when he invited the Suttons to sit and thanked them for their journey. Joining the conference were Secretary of State Monroe and Secretary of the Navy Paul Hamilton.

"You have seen the public response to what they believe happened, Mister Sutton," Madison said. "Please tell us the facts."

Albert related the story from beginning to end, neither dramatizing nor playing down the sequence of events that led to the dismasting of the *Heart of Allegiance* and the death of the sailor.

"And is there any substance to the threat to seize William and try him for treason?" Secretary Monroe asked.

Grandfather Sutton replied, "We don't think so. Our enemies in London got what they wanted by seizing Sutton Shipping. Indeed, our flight to America seems to have proven my guilt. Taking William or myself back would necessitate a trial and awkward questions would be posed."

"Yet it is the position of Great Britain that someone born under English law can never escape his duties to the Crown, even though a naturalized citizen of another country," suggested Hamilton. "Isn't that precisely the law by which they seize American sailors who may have been born English?"

Grandfather Sutton acknowledged the truth of the assertion, then added, "But carried to the extreme, all those born in British America before England recognized our independence would be similarly subject to arrest and impressment."

Albert noted the stress his grandfather laid on the phrase *our independence*. "And a question for *you* if I may, Mister President," Albert said. "The rumors about what happened to *Allegiance* were not accidents, were they?"

"No," Madison admitted. "Speaker Henry Clay and other of the war hawks have seized upon and embellished this outrage in order to increase the pressure for war . . . as they have been doing at every opportunity since last November. But what they did not realize was that embellishment was unnecessary. I have already decided to send to Congress a report suggesting that all diplomatic solutions have been exhausted."

Secretary Monroe's eyes penetrated Albert. "And you, Mister Sutton, will remain in the capital to convince any remaining skeptics?"

Albert bowed and acquiesced.

The morning of June 18, 1812, dawned bright and clear over Baltimore. Dora was up and dressed before daylight. When Angelique arrived in the Sutton carriage at seven to carry the two women to the market square, she was standing on the front stoop, impatiently waiting.

Hooey, the free black manservant of Grandfather Sutton, drove the carriage. The top was down. Angelique sat basking in the sunlight.

"Another letter from Albert, *cherie*!" she said, waving the envelope. "From Washington. This very day he predicts will come the war." She seemed pleased by the news.

Dora squinted and simply greeted her sister-in-law as a reply.

"This does not please you?" Angelique asked.

"I wish there were another way."

"And who does not? But we shall teach the savages in London a lesson, no? As they are giving weapons to the Indians on our western frontier, we shall scourge them for all their wrongs."

"I wish William were home."

"Of course. Albert writes they'll want him in our navy. To fight the scurvy Englishmen."

"Not home to fight," Dora explained. "Just safely home."

Angelique gave a Gallic shrug and fell silent for the ride to market. It was plain Dora did not want to discuss it further.

Dora had grown more uneasy about war and its consequences after seeing the splintered mast of *Allegiance* and the bloodstains of poor, tragic Stephen Birch upon the deck! Somehow the true portent of the conflict had become clear to her in those symbols.

As Baltimore's sentiments rose to fever pitch in favor of battle against England, Dora began to dread the outcome. Not that the English navy did not deserve a good thrashing, but the personal threat against William terrified her. Why had she not considered earlier what war could mean to William's safety? Albert's story about the encounter had roused the fury of every American, but it had turned Dora into a coward.

A war between the United States and Britain would make William more a traitor against the English Crown. And every letter from Albert in Washington indicated that President Madison's declaration would soon be passed in Congress.

William, whether in Portugal or sailing on the high seas, would not hear news of the event until weeks after it became a reality. Unaware of the British attack against *Allegiance* or the outbreak of open hostilities that followed, William could not know of the danger to his life. How often Dora had seen him shake the hand of an English sailor and join in friendly banter about London and the latest escapades of the Prince Regent. What if he offered his hand in friendship, only to be bound with chains and imprisoned? Then tried in an English court and hanged?

Dora had witnessed a hanging at Tyburn in London as a child. Lately, her nightmares had given the dead man William's face.

She regretted her defense of sailors' rights if it led to killing. Helpless and confused, Dora could no longer speak with certainty about right and wrong, justice or right. The only issue that mattered to her was that William return home before the declaration of war was passed by Congress.

The *Julia* leaned hard into the swells as Captain Drake laid her on the starboard tack. William, bracing himself with an arm through a backstay, stood with his face to the salt spray. Though he had no duties that required his presence on deck, he often spent days and nights there. The sea *was* his first love, he thought, while listening to one of the sailors play a Spanish love song on the guitar. Sunlight diffused by the sails warmed his face. The heat was balanced by the cool ocean breeze and spray that misted him from time to time. He dozed in and out of consciousness, contented and free from the worries of the world.

William found himself staring up at the complex web of rigging that allowed the clipper to do the amazing thing that it did: to sail; to harness the wind and travel anywhere. His thoughts turned to his son, Billy. One day he would take him on one of these adventures. He caught sight of a long plume of smoke high on the horizon and followed it down to where it met with a distant ship.

Eyeing the faraway vessel, William determined it to be a whaler, first by the smoky trail, then by the bulbous bow where barrels of whale oil would be stored. Off the side hung the half-stripped carcass of a whale.

"William," Drake's voice from the helm interrupted. "A whaler off portside about a mile."

"I see it, Captain. Let us see what news they bring from Europe."

"Aye-aye," was the response.

A few brisk commands and sailors flew into action, bringing *Julia* about. After the flurry the sails were backed, and in no time the two ships drifted slowly up alongside one another.

William hailed from the portside rail. "What ship are you?"

The whaler's captain called through a speaking trumpet, "*Prometheus*. Out of Bristol ten days ago."

"You've made quick work then."

The captain leaned over to examine the catch hanging from the side. "Yes. I hope it will be the good start of our two-year voyage."

William smiled at the early success, though inside he was glad not to be aboard on the tenth day of a two-year cruise with the reek of blubber and the slime of whale oil. The wind shifted, and he fanned away the foul stench. "What news have you from England then?"

The bearded captain grinned toothlessly. "Ha! Ye are American, are ye not?"

"Indeed."

"Well, I have some news that will smooth yer course. England has revoked the Orders in Council!"

"Hurray!" William shouted. "There shall be no war between England and America!"

The gruff-looking captain bobbed his head. "It seems as though His Majesty has enough on his hands with Old Boney to worry about a parcel of angry colonists."

William shouted for joy again.

The noise was enough that Gerald Fussel, still struggling with seasickness, emerged from below. "What is this about?"

William hurried to Fussel, grabbing his hands and dragging him on deck. Dancing around him in circles, William cried, "No war, Gerald! There will be no war with England."

Gerald caught the spirit. "And that means money!" he cried. "We'll be rich, William!"

"Thanks for the news," William called to *Prometheus*'s captain.

"A pleasure," the whaling officer cried, tipping his hat. "Happy sailing to ye."

"And a profitable voyage to you," was William's response as the vessels drifted on past one another. "Captain!" William cried to Drake. "Tell the cook, tonight we will feast all hands in celebration. There will be no war with Mother England!"

CHAPTER 4

Holding a lavender-scented kerchief to her nose, Dora followed Angelique through the fish market. Dora had grown up in a rural English village where food had been brought to her father's vicarage as a tithe to the church. She had never learned to savor the bustle of the Baltimore seaport market or dickering over the price and quality of goods.

Unlike Dora, Angelique did not cover her nose from the assault of strong smells. What was true in the enormous markets of Paris was true on a warm summer morning in Baltimore, Angelique explained. Using her sense of smell was the surest way she could be certain to choose the freshest fish, other meat, and vegetables on display in the open stalls. She enjoyed bargaining over the price of everything.

With a practiced eye she scrutinized the weighing of every morsel to make sure the scales were true. From the beginning Angelique had taken Dora along twice a week under the guise of teaching her to hold her own with the merchants. Yet six years later, Dora simply imitated her sister-in-law, purchasing her provisions for identical terms.

Hooey followed after the two shoppers, toting the packages in a large wicker basket. The old man had been a houseslave on a Georgia plantation thirty years ago, Dora knew. He had been brought on a blackbirder from the Ivory Coast as a child and bought and sold a half-dozen times before he was finally given to Grandfather Sutton in payment of a debt and then was given his freedom. After that, Hooey stayed on with Grandfather Sutton. Although still a servant, Hooey carried himself with a new dignity as a freeman.

Dora stood before a stall containing a cartload of plums. Angelique was uninterested, which left the responsibility of the purchase on Dora.

"Buy plums! First plums of the summer! Fresh sweet plums! Plums here!" the vendor cried. "Penny a pound! Penny a pound! Fresh plums!"

"Lovely," she ventured as the grizzled seller glanced her way.

"Can't find better, madam! Nowheres in all the States!"

"Penny a pound?" she queried.

"Aye. Not a better price in Baltimore!"

Hooey cleared his throat and stuck out his lower lip in disagreement. Dora heard the warning and whispered to the aged freeman, "Are they not the best bargain?"

Hooey said in her ear, "He put his thumb on de scale when he weigh. Make his half pound be a pound, see? So Missus Angelique walk on by."

Dora's face fell. Would she never learn to look for such things?

The vendor's expression clouded. "Here now. What's that yaller-eyed darkie tellin' you?"

Dora stammered, "That . . . we . . . I have plums in the cellar." This was not entirely a lie. She had jars of plum preserves remaining from last year.

But the merchant knew Hooey had witnessed his deception. For an instant Dora thought he would argue with her that no one had plums except for himself. Instead he eyed the manservant with a harsh look to warn him not to share the crooked secret with any other potential customers. Hooey wisely kept his eyes lowered on the bundles in the basket as Dora hurried after Angelique.

"Thank you, Hooey," Dora said, breathing a sigh of relief.

The old man shrugged. "Plenty plums comin' August. He speakin' Choctaw. A babirusa, he is. You wait. No use payin' double to de likes of dat kine."

Ahead Angelique picked her way from one stall to another as beyond them the staccato calling of the slave auctioneer drummed unendingly over the hubbub of the crowd. Only once, Dora noticed, did Hooey look toward the auction block when a woman and her infant child were carried weeping to the platform as two of her children called for her from a group of chained slaves who had already been sold.

This pitiful spectacle was one more reason Dora hated market day.

"Strong and healthy she is!" The auctioneer waved his hand at the woman. "All her teeth! Virginia born an' raised. Mother to these two fine youngsters just sold there. The babe is a boy child. No doubt will grow into a strong healthy servant." He appealed to the man who had purchased her children. "Will you not buy her and the baby as well, sir?"

The buyer shook his head. "Don't need a baby. Don't want a baby. Only trouble. Likely die anyway.

Take the woman though." The woman began to weep and plead, and her two older children began screaming for her not to leave them. In the end, no one bid on the mother until the auctioneer received a nod from her present owner, and permission was given to sell the baby separately and cheaply.

"Do I hear twenty dollars for this fine female?"

"Please, no!" cried the woman slave. "He ain't but a month old! He die if he ain't got no mama to feed him!"

The buyer shouted, "I'll have the woman, but I got no place for a squalling babe for her to care for too. She'll have work to do. No time for that!"

Angelique, a sour look on her face, turned away from a heap of onions. "Pity sake!" she exclaimed. "Have they no mercy?"

Others in the marketplace glanced toward the ruckus. The bidding for the mother rose to forty-five dollars without the burden of her infant.

Dora stood transfixed as the mother was sold to the same man who had purchased her two older children. There was horrible mercy in that. At least the woman would be with those two. But what about the baby? Who would want a slave child one month in age?

Then bidders milled uneasily as the tiny child

was placed in a basket and held up by the auctioneer.

"What am I bid?"

From the back of the crowd someone shouted, "It'll die anyways. Might as well put it in a sack and throw it in the bay!"

Inexplicably, Dora found herself pushing fiercely through the crowd with Angelique and Hooey close on her heels.

She heard a voice cry, "ONE DOLLAR FOR THE BABY!"

It was her own voice. Had she ever shouted so loudly? With such anguish? Heads pivoted to see who had made the bid. She raised her hand high. "I'LL BUY HIM!"

"It's William Sutton's wife," someone cried in astonishment.

The auctioneer chortled, tossed the basket into the air, and caught it. A weak cry emanated from within.

"Missus Dora Sutton, is it?" the fellow said with amusement.

Snickering rose from the bidders, and from the fringe a male voice shouted, "I'll give you two dollars, Ben! Then I'll toss the thing off the pier myself!"

Frantic, Dora countered, "THREE DOLLARS!"

"Four! I'll get it back when we wager how long it'll take to drown **the** thing!"

"FIVE!"

"Six. And we'll chuck it off right now!"

Tears of fury stung her eyes at the cruel sport of these heartless men.

"SEVEN DOLLARS!" She rushed toward the steps of the platform as men mocked her.

The auctioneer cocked an eyebrow at her as she approached. "Seven American dollars from the good Missus Sutton! As much as for these two half-grow'd niggers just sold here! Well, **well**. Seems the lady is determined to ruin Mister Carbury's sport. Will you bid eight dollars, Mister Carbury?" A roar of merriment greeted her as she reached the top step, ran to the auctioneer, and snatched the wicker basket from him.

She lowered her voice. "My husband shall hear how you have used me as the butt of your joke today."

His grin faltered. "Seven dollars," he repeated dryly.

"Seven it is." She looked down at the tiny, naked baby wailing in the basket. There was not so much as a rag between the skin of the newborn and the rough weave of the container.

The auctioneer raised his hand. "SOLD! One infant . . . newborn . . . slave for SEVEN DOLLARS to Missus Sutton!"

Cheers and hoots resounded.

The auctioneer lowered his face near to her as she counted out the currency. "Of course, we make no guarantees about the health of any of our merchandise. Can't live without mother's milk. It'll be dead before next market day, ma'am. A waste of good money is what your husband will say."

The ride back home from the market passed in stony silence between Dora and Angelique. The baby, feeble, filthy, and caked with muck, lay wrapped in Dora's yellow silk shawl in the basket on the seat beside Dora. She felt sick, grieved for the poor woman whose child she had bought and terrified that perhaps she would not be able to keep him alive.

The sun was high, and Hooey had raised the top to shield the women and infant against the heat. Angelique, cheek in hand, stared gloomily out at the streets as they rode toward Cathedral Hill.

At last Dora spoke. "Won't you say something? Anything?"

Angelique glanced at her and then away. "Dora."
Such disapproval in the tone of a single word!

"What else could I do?"

With a sigh, Angelique replied, "Since you are
Dora, there was nothing else."

"You heard what they wanted to do!"

"They would not have . . . it was a game. To
entrap a foolish woman."

"Cruel."

"On that we agree."

"He would have died."

"He probably will anyway. Have you thought
what . . . how we are to feed him? Last year I might
have nursed him. But my petite jewel is weaned.
My milk is dried up."

"We'll find a nurse."

"*Mon Dieu!* Dora, you are a fool!"

Dora stared at the minute, clenched fist of the
child. "I had to."

"I know. And if you had not, *ma cherie*, I myself
would have. But! *Mon Dieu!* Seven dollars!"

"But you heard . . ."

"They would have given him away. It was to
make you frantic that the fellow bid so. But what
does one expect from someone who stopped to
gaze upon the season's first plums stacked in the

stall of the market's worst villain? Such babies as this have hardly any chance to live, *cherie*! Baltimore has hundreds of such as these. Many colors to choose from. Free."

Dora nodded. "When I was young there was a boy in our village. His father was a sea captain who brought him a snake from somewhere. Well, the boy carried the thing round his neck like a string of glass beads. He fed it baby chicks. And one day he showed me. I saw the chick huddled in the corner, petrified. I cried, and the boy said if I gave him a penny he would give me the chick."

"And you gave him a penny?"

"Every week. He showed me the chick in the box with his creature, and I ran crying to fetch my penny."

"How many weeks did this terrible thing go on?"

"Twelve."

"Did the snake die?"

"No. I'm sure he fed it other chicks when I was not there."

"Then what stopped it?"

"Father. He would not give me any more pennies. Baby chicks were ten a penny then. I suppose the brute supported the snake on what I paid for one chick."

Angelique softened. She leaned forward to look at the baby. "Ah, Dora. The slavers, *ma cherie*! They have the heart of that dreadful boy, I fear! And you . . . you remain tender Dora."

"Help me think. What shall we do?"

"We must find a wet nurse. Soon. Look how dry and drawn his flesh is? Perhaps he has not eaten in some time. And see there how he puts his tiny fist to his mouth. Oh! Sweet little bird. You are hungry, are you not?" Angelique turned worried eyes toward Dora. "Guard your heart, *Cherie*," she said. "This little bird is near to flying away."

CHAPTER 5

Twelve hundred miles across the blue Atlantic waters, the westerly winds carried the *Julia* to Portugal in fourteen days. Captain Drake's stars and charts had not been wrong, for when the ship emerged from the haze, the first sight of land included the wide mouth of the olive-green Tagus River. Another eight miles past steep, bushy hillsides to where the river widened, was Lisbon, Portugal.

From the foredeck of *Julia*, William surveyed the scenery. Ships of all sizes with sails in almost an equal variety of colors littered the waters like a sky full of kites. Portuguese falluas competed for space with North African xebecs and Dutch schouws. The noon sun warmed the waters, casting a million sparkling mirrors. In the shallows fishermen hauled in sardine nets, while nearby, on the land, ancient houses and rubble-strewn battlements paved the shore from waterfront to hilltop.

As the *Julia* coasted gently into port, Fussel joined William on the bow. "I hear this place has quite a history."

Inspecting the serene, Old World beauty of Lisbon and the bay, William paused before replying. "It is so different from America," he murmured, "where everything is new. It's as if Lisbon is stuck in time."

Fussel interjected, "And what a lot of time to be stuck in! Our host, Senhor Braganza, tells me that three or more thousand years ago the Phoenicians called this place *Alis Ubbo*, meanin' 'delightful shore.'"

"That it is," William added as he disembarked the ship.

Immediately upon setting foot on land William was surrounded by peddlers hawking clothing, blankets, fresh fish, and ceramic pottery. He could not speak the language, compounded of Greek, low Latin, French, Moorish, and highly influenced by Celtic. The dialect there was as multihued as the tile mosaics that covered the walls, and William became lost in the sounds of those who would have him buy their goods.

Gerald Fussel, who pretended to know many

languages from around the globe, stepped between William and the dockside traders. In loud English and a fractured smattering of Creole French and Spanish he rambled about nothing, but his impassioned gestures communicated his order to go away, and the vendors soon left the two men alone.

Shortly after they found a carriage that would take them to Carlos Braganza's palace. Up the hill they rattled, passing elaborate, whitewashed, meandering mansions that contrasted splendid elegance with massive piles of rubble and ruin. At one of the highest points of the city, called *Castelo de Sao Jorge*, William could take in the entire city at once. Winding back down the other side, Fussel announced that the Braganza estate was in Alfama, the easternmost and also oldest quarter of Lisbon.

Fussel told William more about their host on their way up the windy stone streets. "He's a wealthy man, as you might expect from one who finances expensive voyages, but his fortune is more vast than you can imagine. Related to the Portuguese royal family, Carlos has taken his share and with shrewd business sense turned it into what might be a million-dollar fortune, though he isn't sayin'. Plays his cards close, does Carlos Braganza."

William, fascinated with the city, was not

impressed with Fussel's claims of the Braganza fortune until a brace of liveried servants in powdered wigs sprinted from a gatehouse to let the carriage turn into a succession of lavish gardens and marble terraces. The sight of the house itself was more like a view of Canterbury Cathedral: huge walls suspended the stone tracery around massive panes of stained glass. In the shady, mossy courtyards patinaed bronze statues adorned granite fountains in which goldfish darted.

A short uniformed man with a tanned, wrinkled face let them out of the cab. Recognizing Gerald Fussel, the servant bowed. "You are earlier than expected." The man's English was broken and heavily accented.

In a booming voice, Fussel explained, "Yes, the westerlies were strong and straight. We had no quarrels with the sea."

"*Excellentissimo*! Senhor Braganza will be most pleased to see you. But first let me to your rooms take you."

"Good!" Fussel bellowed at a volume that made William worry of awakening ghosts in the hushed surroundings.

"I am William Sutton," William offered in a softer tone.

The older man waved slowly, nodding twice. "To your rooms then."

William stepped through the elaborately carved stone doorway and into the world of Carlos Braganza.

After two wrong turns on the way from his bedroom, William halted uncertainly at the door of a long, narrow study paved with massive slate tiles, and lined with richly ornamented antique bookshelves. At its far end, Gerald Fussel sat talking to a short man behind a disproportionately dominant leather-topped desk. Afternoon light, cut into slits by wooden shutters, warmed the otherwise dim, serious room.

Leaning forward slightly and perching on the edge of his seat, Fussel spoke eagerly to the man. "As I say, Carlos, since the comin' of the cotton gin, there are not markets enough for the amount of product the South has available."

Spare of stature and hair, and glowing with a Mediterranean tan, Carlos Braganza interjected, "Yes, but you need not worry for that. That is Carlos Braganza's business. With the European war disruptive of trade, Britain and France have not been able to get enough material for clothing, and their problem requires my answer. Though we are grateful for England's protection against the monster Bonaparte, technically as a neutral I can supply them both."

Fussel furrowed his bushy brows, and then said, "But what of the royal family's flight to Brazil? They have just returned and may disapprove of trade with France."

Braganza's confident tone accepted no anxiety. "There is no need for me to worry. I am myself merely once removed from royalty. It is a critical distinction, for had I been closer to the succession, I might have fled also and not had the opportunity to acquire the resources I used to propel myself to where we are today. And yet my connections are sure protection from criticism in Portugal. As for outside my country," Braganza said, shrugging, "Napoleon has needs and will not quibble if we are supplying Britain too. If he does, then he will cut his own throat. Likewise Britain, though disapproving, must . . . how does the English go? *Turn a blind eye*, for we allowed them refuge here when French forces drove them out of Spain."

Fussel, absently weighing a gold filigreed cigar case and studying an ivory-handled penknife, nodded. "That's for cotton," Fussel concluded. "And what of the black ivory you say needs transportin'?"

Braganza did not answer. His face lit up and he rose from his chair. "William Sutton!"

Swiveling his bulk awkwardly around in the too-slender chair, Fussel faced the arched doorway in which William stood combed, shaved, and dressed in clean clothes.

"Senhor Braganza, I presume?" William said, extending his hand.

Braganza rounded the desk, making his way to the middle of the room with hands outstretched to embrace. "William," he said warmly. "You have grown up since last I saw you! How long ago? So many years ago in England."

William recollected the radiant face of this man, much younger then, with more hair. But his vibrant features and intense looks remained. "How wonderful to see you! I had almost forgotten our brief encounter when I was a boy of nine or ten."

The two men clasped each other's shoulders. William recalled how Braganza had made him feel welcome when Grandfather Sutton had been short with him for interrupting a business meeting.

"I was yet a young man myself. I could not have been older than you are now when I was sent by my uncle to England to acquire my first cargo of English wool." He paused, turning his flushed expression of pleasure toward Gerald Fussel. "You had written to say that our dealings would be with a family of Suttons, but since it was America, I had not made the connection."

Fussel edged farther out on his seat until his gigantic belly looked dangerously close to dragging him down to the slates. "I had no idea either."

With a tanned arm around his back, Carlos Braganza walked William through a set of large open doors. Red Spanish tiles paved an expansive patio surrounded by lush, tropical gardens. Uninvited, Fussel stood and awkwardly followed. When he caught Braganza's eye, he placed his hand against his mouth in a warning gesture, rapidly dropped when William turned.

"Well then," Braganza continued easily, "we were speaking of the transportation of cotton. Gerald tells me your fastest ship is called the *Julia*?"

"After my late mother, yes."

"I am sorry to hear of that," Braganza offered gravely. "But the choice of names is a fortuitous one. Did Gerald not tell you? Lisbon was once styled by the Romans, *Feliciatas Julia*."

William chuckled at the coincidence.

"And so we speak of the market for cotton," Braganza said expansively, "and since there is such a need, we may fulfill as many orders as we can find ships for."

"I'm sure you have heard about the impressment of our sailors and the dangers associated with shipping," William cautioned. "It is practically impossible for a man to afford insurance. The indemnity of a single cargo has risen to one third its value."

The three men stopped by a rail fence that separated groomed grounds from flower-covered hills.

"But this is no concern for Braganza! With the money he will make, he will pay you double your profits. Particularly as the labor cost will be slight."

Fussel shot another cautionary glare at the host.

Before William could ask for an explanation, a woman's voice called out, "Papa," in a peremptory tone and repeated it several more times before she was visible.

The three men spun round in unison, questions on their faces.

The speaker emerged from Braganza's office and marched toward the men. Her hair was chocolate-brown and her eyes the most beautiful hazel William had ever seen. The young woman of about twenty wore her hair up, above a ruffled white silk shirt. Sable leather riding pants with silver buckles and tassels down the side of each leg completed the equestrian costume. Her words, though spoken in Portuguese, were clearly angry.

Carlos fanned at her and answered soothingly, "Michelle, Michelle. We have visitors from America."

Michelle Braganza frowned at Fussel and at William, who stared back wide-eyed, madly entangled in her beauty.

"My dear," Braganza said, as if to make clear his thoughts, "you must speak in English in front of our visitors."

Sighing as if she did not have time for such idleness, Michelle continued, "Papa, the idiots who are feeding my horse have left the stable door unlatched, and he has opened it again!"

"Her horse, he is very smart," Carlos interjected to William.

"He is thrashing around on the floor in the stables and throwing his head," she exclaimed. "I do not know what to do!"

"Did you speak with Diego? Surely he will know what to do."

"He is gone today," she said defiantly, stomping her foot, "and no one knows anything!"

William stepped forward, interrupting her. "He is colicking."

"What?" she cried. "You know of this horse sickness?"

"Yes," William replied simply. "He must have gotten into the grain bin. It is often fatal," he added.

"Fatal! Hurry! You must come with me at once." Michelle grabbed William's arm.

Braganza protested, "I'm sorry, dear, but he cannot. We are discussing important matters."

William spoke up. "No sir, there can be no more important matters right now than your daughter's horse. I will help her, and we can resume later."

"Ah, Michelle, you have made a conquest I think," Braganza teased. He turned to William, who blushed. "There is no better way to a man's heart than to first make his daughter happy. Go then. We will talk when you return."

Wasting no time, the sparkling and imperious Michelle tugged William by hand and heart, rushing him around the house and down to the stables.

William could hear the thrashing before he ever reached the stable: wallboards were banging and upright posts cracking.

Michelle, almost in tears, pleaded with William and clutched his sleeve, as if she thought him about to change his mind and desert her. "Thunder will tear himself to pieces if he is not controlled. I tried to talk to him, to grab him, but I could not!"

"No, you mustn't," he warned. "A colicking horse is in serious pain, and when they go to thrashing, they know how to do nothing gently."

She began to cry aloud, causing William to realize maybe it would be better if he did not talk to her about it.

They rounded the whitewashed, smooth-mortared front of the row of stables. William did not have to ask where the horse was; he followed his ears. "Get a bridle," he instructed with the calm assurance of an admiral going into battle.

"A what?" Michelle asked through the liquid streaming down her cheeks.

William was struck again by how extraordinarily beautiful she was even when crying. He stepped toward her, thinking he would embrace her, comfort her. Just as quickly he shook the idea from his mind. "Harness and lead rope," he said brusquely. "Now!"

"Oh, yes!" She hurried off to another room to get them.

A dust cloud choked William. Upon entering

the main storeroom of the stalls, he could see everything was in shambles. Barrels of grain had been kicked in, smashed to little more than metal rings, strips of wood, and piles of sweet grain. Hay had been cleared from the center of a ring and piled around the thrashing beast in a large circle as he rolled back and forth.

Michelle returned with the tack. William took it, then stood wondering how he would get control of this horse. He knew that if he did not get the animal to its feet the writhing agony would twist its intestines into impenetrable, fatal knots. He addressed Michelle. "'Thunder,' you say?"

She nodded, bleary-eyed and hiccuping softly.

Thunder reminded William of his old horse Powder, able to dash off in a flash and the wildest ride he had ever seen. Like his favorite mount, abandoned when they fled England, this was an exceptional animal and one worth saving.

He approached with apprehension. Staying close to the head was vital if William was to avoid being rolled on or lashed out at by a flailing hoof. He must attach the harness and prevent the beast from spinning.

Holding the harness upside down so the throat strap was up and away, William moved in low and cautious. Thunder sensed someone was there and desisted in his buffeting, but as soon as William was close enough to slip the bridle over the head, the horse vaulted off the ground.

The tip of the animal's nose smacked William in the forehead. William saw stars and tasted the metallic sensation of blood. He flew backward, crashing into pieces of barrel, and was blinded temporarily. When his sight came back to him, William's first thought was to see if Michelle was concerned for him.

"Go get him," the woman insisted, "before he tears himself to pieces."

William charged the beast. This time, latching onto Thunder's head, William found himself in a seated position, holding on as best he could. Thunder thrashed him from side to side. William felt and looked like a man hanging on to the bowsprit on the prow of a ship tossed in a severe storm.

Gripping the animal's nose and waiting for the space between lunges, William seized the moment when he could slip the harness on. He had to fight with the buckle. Another instant later the right lull came for the strap to be threaded and the buckle slotted tight.

"Now to get Thunder to his feet!" William

yelled, wrestling the horse over to a crouch on its belly. Then in one motion, uniting the strength of legs, back, and arms, he raised the horse's head, and the body followed.

Before Michelle had blinked, William had completed the task. "Oh, thank God," she cried, looking at her dirt-caked, wild-eyed horse.

"Move aside!" William commanded. "We must get this horse out into the sunlight where he can be walked."

Thunder dragged his feet and attempted to sit down. William whipped the creature across the rump with the rope end, and Thunder bucked. "Go get a large jug of olive oil," William ordered.

Michelle started to ask why but was cut off as William issued the order a second time.

Leading the horse over to a high fence, William clambered up the side with the rope in hand. Yanking the rope taut so that the animal's chin hung over the boards, William wrapped the cord around a post several times.

Michelle returned with a crock of oil.

"Give it to me."

The Braganza heiress appeared shocked that William would use such a tone with her. It seemed to William she was not used to receiving orders.

Prying open the mouth of the mahogany animal he poured the contents of the urn down Thunder's throat. The animal coughed and tried to toss his head but could not and gave in to swallowing the green oil.

Baffled, Michelle asked, "Why are you doing this to my horse?"

"It's a lubricant for that grain he's eaten. If it should enter his intestines without this oil, as some already has, the grain will swell and cause his insides to burst."

More worried-looking than before, Michelle said, "Well, hurry up! Pour some more."

Soon the jar was empty, and Thunder was tired. He tried to slide down to his haunches while still strung on the fence. "No, no, boy!" William insisted. "It's time to walk."

Thunder hung from the fence with all of his weight and sounded as if he were choking. The rope was so clenched that it was impossible to undo it. Michelle watched with fascination as William spun and spotted an ax in a woodpile. Sprinting to it, he yanked it from the round and hurried back. Then, in one swooping motion, William hacked the fence post in two, freeing the knot. The rope flew up in the air, and the horse dropped to his knees.

Wasting no time, William rounded the fence, and before Thunder had time to lie down again, William had him up and walking.

Michelle watched with concern for a long time. For the first hour, she could not take her eyes off her pet. Then, as time dragged on, William found her sitting on a bale of straw, following his every move with her magnetic brownish-green eyes. Neither had said a word.

"Your head," Michelle said at last, pointing to the swollen, shiny knot on William's forehead.

"It's nothing," he replied before fingering the purple, egg-sized lump. "Perhaps it was more than I'd noticed."

"Let me get you a compress for it," Michelle offered.

"It's fine, really."

She insisted it was not and hurried off again, this time returning with cool, wet cloths. "How is Thunder doing?" she asked, while gently placing the towels on William's head.

"Doing well," William replied, looking back at the sleepy animal plodding at the end of the lead rope. "He seems to have gotten the hang of it. Hasn't tried to lie down again."

Michelle petted the animal lovingly. "That's

because Thunder is a smart horse. Maybe too smart."

William agreed. "A couple more hours of this."

"Why so long, Senhor William?"

William was shocked to hear her say his name. Her breathy accent enchanted him.

At first lost for words, he finally explained that standing would be dangerous, for the animal might want to lie down. There was yet a danger of a twisted gut until Thunder showed he could pass droppings again. Only then would he be out of danger.

Carlos Braganza appeared, or at least his head showed above the boards, followed by Gerald Fussel. "Senhor William, your reinforcements are here."

A moment later a wiry servant dressed in the shapeless clothes and boots of a working man arrived. As soon as Michelle saw him she launched into a flurry of Portuguese. "Diego" was the sole part William understood, but he gathered this must be the unlucky stablehand who forgot to lock the stall.

Diego ducked beneath the force of Michelle's tirade. With his head bowed almost to the ground, the servant took the rope from William and began walking the horse, while the other four adjourned to the mansion.

William was writing in his diary after dawn the next day when he heard a knock at his bedroom door.

"Senhor William?" the voice of Carlos Braganza called respectfully.

William put down his quill pen, examined his ink-stained fingers, and decided there was no easy remedy to clean him up speedily. "Yes, Senhor Braganza. Come in."

Braganza was polite. "I hope I am not bothering you by coming this early. Manuel said you rang for a pot of chocolate, so I knew you were awake."

"No bother, Senhor," was William's reply. "What can I do for you?"

Sitting down on the corner of the bed nearest the desk, Braganza explained. "Word has come to me that I am to send food and other provisions to the northern coast of Spain immediately; to the Spanish guerrillas fighting against Emperor Napoleon. The freight is ready to be loaded; however, not a single one of my ships is in port at this time. The one I am awaiting is two days late, and I fear it may have come to harm somewhere."

William read into Braganza's mind and jumped to the conclusion of the visit. "And you need me to run this load for you?"

Senhor Braganza sighed as if it were too much to ask. "Would you consider undertaking it, Senhor William? It is of tremendous importance to me, or I would not ask it."

Carlos Braganza was a man William felt he would do anything for, though he did not run from speaking the truth to him either. "I understand all supplies for the guerrillas must be cleared through British headquarters. This will be an extremely dangerous mission, heading north to a Spanish harbor, what with the British blockade and the French in opposition as well. Where did you say the cargo was to make port?"

With hands clasped, Braganza said imploringly, "Just to the city of Vitorio."

"That is very near the French. I would be running the risk of being suspected by both sides of supplying their enemy."

Carlos indicated his understanding.

"I could be impressed, or worse, hanged for treason if the Royal Navy suspected me of aiding the French."

"I have a plan where if you are stopped, you

will produce fake documents stating that these supplies are for Wellington's troops in Corunna. They will never know the difference."

"And what if they happen to see me going the wrong way?"

"You will then tell them you ran into French privateers and had to flee."

William thought long and hard before shaking his head. "I do not sense the security here that I do when sailing the American coast. My ship could be taken."

"I understand, and for this danger you will be handsomely paid."

"There is so much at risk . . ."

Braganza interrupted. "I understand, William. I should not have asked. Please excuse me." He stood and walked to the door. "Though I would have paid you double the tariff in gold sovereigns." He turned to see William's reaction.

Consideration was written large on William's brow, as the wind of ambition filled the sails of the mind. *Gold coins,* he thought, *double the tariff.* "A brief trip?"

"Two and a half to three days each way at the most?

"The documents are ready?"

"Being prepared as we speak. In fact, I also had my forger make substitute American papers for you so no one will recognize your name. William Summerset. It is a nice American name, yes?"

"Summerset, Summerset," William parroted as he pondered the name. "It will do. And what of the name and history of my ship?"

"Artificial logbooks are being created. You have sailed from Carolina to Brazil to Lisbon aboard the *Feliciatas Julia*."

William chuckled at the simple name change. "Bravo!" he applauded. "When are we to get under way?"

Braganza's eyes brightened. "Soon. A week at most."

Both stood as Braganza offered his hand. William grasped it vigorously.

"You are a good man, William Summerset," Braganza said with a chuckle. "When you return, you must go riding with my daughter. She has never spoken highly of any man before, nor found one she thought to be a worthy riding companion."

A warm sensation passed through William's body. He began to blush and sweat as he thought of Dora back in the States. Business subterfuge was one thing, but he should not let any misunderstanding about his marriage remain. "I'm honored, but really . . ."

"Ah, you needn't be modest. Maybe we make you son of Carlos." Braganza displayed a set of dazzlingly white teeth. "Yes. You are worthy."

Lost for words, William sputtered and could not make his lips form the words he knew he should utter.

Taking William's confusion for embarrassment, Braganza said, "It is all right. I don't mean to alarm you! Please, return to what you are doing and soon we will eat." He patted William on the shoulder, bowed slightly, and left the room.

William exhaled as a wave of exhaustion washed over him. *Such a persuasive man,* he thought. *First I say yes to the most dangerous mission of my life, and then he throws his daughter at me. What am I to do?*

Though Albert remained in Washington as an unpaid assistant to Secretary Monroe, he despaired of ever being able to fathom the American political mind.

True, the Congress had passed President Madison's declaration of war with the vocal and sometimes physical support of the populace, but it had not been a resounding endorsement. The vote had been seventy-nine to forty-nine in the House and nineteen to thirteen in the Senate; hardly a united front to take on the might of Britain. The majority of the dissenters were New Englanders, more interested in trade than patriotism (like his brother, Albert had to admit). There was a smattering of talk of secession in the New England states.

Of course, this blasé attitude to war had its counterpoise in the motives of those who desired war for their own ends: the Westerners who wanted to punish the Indians and push back the American frontier, and the war hawks who favored an invasion of Canada.

It was a pity that communications between the Old World and the New were so sluggish. The Americans were counting on the fact that Britain was too engaged with fighting Napoleon to mount an effective campaign against the United States.

"Albert," Secretary Monroe said, tapping on the doorframe of his assistant's office, "it has been suggested that you lead a delegation to French Canada to see if they will join us in fighting Britain. Will you go?"

Aghast, Albert replied, "Is this an order or a request? I am, as you know, regarded as a traitor to

France. Besides, who has said that the Quebecois are interested in getting into our war? This is not to their interests, I think. And we cannot raise an army here, let alone in another country."

"It's true," Monroe conceded. "Even the war hawks among the state governors promise only *handfuls* of militiamen, and deliver fewer. Actually, I did not want you to go. I think you and I are needed here. We seem to be the only two who expect the British to attack *us*."

Shaking his head with exasperation, Albert concurred. "Your countrymen . . . pardon, *our* countrymen, think of war as a grand game to be won by threats and speeches. They have not seen the reality as I have. The British will come, monsieur. Assuredly, they will come."

"I know. That is why you and I must discuss seriously where *they* will hit *us*."

CHAPTER 6

Despite all of Dora's care and prayer, the newborn black child died in two days. The Sutton family physician, Dr. Polson, declared that nothing more could have been done.

Grieving and brooding about penny chicks the entire week, Dora could not shake the thought she had to do something about the horrible problem. As yet, however, she was at a loss for any possible solution.

At Sunday service, after the opening hymns and prayer, Assistant Vicar Sheffield took the pulpit.

"We take our lesson this morning from the Book of St. Luke, chapter eighteen, verses one through eight: 'Then He spoke a parable to them, that men always ought to pray and not lose heart, saying: "There was in a certain city a judge who did not fear God nor regard man. Now there was a widow in that city; and she came to him, saying, 'Get justice for me from my adversary.' And he would not for a while; but afterward he said within himself, 'Though I do not fear God nor regard man, yet because this widow troubles me I will avenge her, lest by her continual coming she weary me.'"

"Then the Lord said, 'Hear what the unjust judge said. And shall God not avenge His own elect who cry out day and night to Him, though He bears long with them? I tell you that He will avenge them speedily. Nevertheless, when the Son of Man comes, will He really find faith on the earth?'"

"This is the Word of the Lord. Amen."

Dora found her troubled dreams about changing the world compounded with the Scripture reading. To hide her dismay, she turned and appeared to stare absently out the window. But the roaring in her ears did not prevent the preacher's words from reaching into her soul.

Vicar Sheffield began again.

"You see, God wants us to seek His will in all things, and He never afflicts our hearts and consciences with trivial concerns. We mortals have a tendency to count on God's miracles, urging Him to solve our problems for us. Instead of praying, 'Thy will be done,' we pray either 'My will be done,' or 'Thy will be altered to suit me!' But God has a different plan in mind. God wants us to heed His voice by lending our feet to the prayers we send toward heaven, by using our muscles to lift the burdens of others."

The vicar had Dora's attention, since through the vicar's words her plan was being formed.

As the service concluded, the congregation trickled out the doors of the church. Dora remained back among the shadows in the foyer.

Finally, as the last member had gone and Vicar Sheffield began to replace the hymnals and prayer books, Dora lifted her chin and strode confidently toward him.

"Vicar Sheffield?" Dora ventured. "I have a matter to discuss with you."

"Why, Missus Sutton. Yes. How are you? What can I do for you?"

"Vicar, I feel . . ." Dora stopped and swallowed, aware that there was a giant commitment in what she was about to say and equally aware that God's will and that of her husband might not, probably would not, coincide. In a rush she said, "I am being led to be of help to the foundlings of this city." She told him about the scene at the slave auction and the death of the unwanted baby.

The vicar raised his bushy brows in surprise and formed his lips into a soundless whistle.

Dora faltered. "I suppose I am merely . . . I just thought that perhaps . . ."

"No. No, my dear. Please go on."

"Well I thought possibly the former parsonage, because it stands empty . . . maybe we could turn it into an orphanage for the abandoned slave infants."

Startled, Vicar Sheffield queried, "Missus Sutton, surely you cannot mean to take in colored babies? Why, half the congregation are slave owners. No. I think not. It wouldn't be wise."

"Yes, Vicar, I understand your position. But surely you can see mine. Helpless infants are being drowned, starved, or left to die because as labor they are useless. But do they not have souls as we do?"

Vicar Sheffield patronizingly grasped her shoulder and began, "Missus Sutton, please. I'm sure your generous heart is genuinely . . ."

"No, Vicar." The boldness of her reply astonished them both but Dora continued, more sure of herself than ever. "Did you not say in your sermon that God will grant us the miracles, but we have to do the work? I am willing, and these are God's children. Would you deny them? Because to do so . . ."

The Vicar held up his hand to cut her off.

"Dora, the implication is clear. To deny them is to deny Christ Himself. You make your case concisely. But you must know that you will face opposition and violent hostility." When Dora remained unblinking, he continued, "I can grant you the old parsonage on these terms: You must secure the funding and workers. We simply do not have in our budget to provide for the foundlings of Baltimore's slaves, nor can we blithely espouse a cause that many of our members will find distasteful. Having said that, and if you are determined to proceed, may God bless your efforts."

Dora smiled broadly, thanked him, surprised the man yet again by embracing him, and hurried from the church to find Angelique.

Eager to share her news, Dora nearly tripped over herself upon entering the parlor of Angelique's house. She was thrilled to find her sister-in-law and Grandfather Sutton chatting idly over tea.

Flushed from the exertion of running, with wisps of hair escaping from her usually well-coifed hair, Dora's appearance worried her relatives.

"*Cherie!*" Angelique exclaimed. "What is it? You look the fright."

"Oh, Angelique! Grandfather! It's marvelous! I know how to help the slave children! No more need to die! I approached the vicar after church, and he is going to let me employ the disused parsonage to house them. An orphanage. I am going to start an orphanage!"

"*C'est possible*? Dora, this was, I thought, but a fancy passing through your brains. You cannot possibly mean to . . ."

"On the contrary, Angelique," Dora said firmly. "I *do* mean to, and I certainly will. I have but one immediate problem."

Angelique and Grandfather Sutton exchanged bewildered glances and then turned back to Dora.

"Pardon," Angelique said evenly. "Go on, *cherie.*"

"The vicar said I must finance and staff the orphanage without the help of the church."

Grandfather Sutton, having remained quiet until now, softly spoke. "My dear Dora, money is it? To establish such a wonderful charity? Then you shall have it. *I* will finance this endeavor for the first months. It is a worthy cause, and it will indeed be an honor to assist you."

Angelique, joining excitedly in Dora's venture, offered, "And I will be about the market to get the things you will need: provisions and nurses, *non*?"

The small enclave huddled together to begin formulating their plans.

The renamed *Feliciatas Julia* cruised down the murky Tagus River at the turn of the tide. From the lake formed near Lisbon where the stream narrowed, the volume of water forced between the banks flowed swiftly. William, traveling with a substitute crew of Portuguese and Spanish sailors had little to do except steer until the olive water swirled into Atlantic blue.

Heading north from Lisbon there was no southerly flow of air to propel the watercraft easily. William was forced to tack far to the west in order to make good against the head wind. This maneuver, while necessary, could add as much as a hundred miles to the trip, though William speculated it might be Providence's way of keeping him away from the coastline where many of the British warships patrolled. No war for Britain and America, but unauthorized trading was treated as smuggling and dealt with harshly. If his luck held, the

English would be coasting down toward the Strait of Gibraltar on the easy inside passage and miss seeing the *Julia* altogether.

After seven hours of sailing and as eight bells announced the end of the second dogwatch, William retired to his cabin to rest. He was not down much more than an hour before he was alerted that his expectation had proven false. There was a banging on the cabin door, followed by a frantic cry. "Mister Summerset! Mister Summerset! A man-of-war has been spotted on the northeastern horizon!"

Having slept in his clothes and boots, William sprang to his feet and was on deck with his spyglass in less than ten seconds. "Why was I not notified of this sooner?" he demanded. Berating himself for replacing his regular crew in the interest of the deception, he asked, "How long have they been keeping this course?"

"Since first sight, Captain. One turn of the glass."

"Blast it!" William smashed the telescope into a burlap sack of dry beans stacked right beside the hatchway. The sharp brass edge of the scope's tube split the fabric in a smiling arc. Beans poured out on the deck at his feet while William debated what to do. Should he turn south and run? But that action would give the game away at once, unless he could convince the Royal Navy that he feared they were French. His mind turned the possibilities over and over in what seemed an eternity but was actually no more than a minute.

William knew what he would have to do: heave-to and allow them aboard. There was no other choice. Here in the war zone bravado appropriate for the high seas did not apply; the warship would smash *Julia* to flinders.

A deckhand removed the bent spyglass from the sack. When he did so, stubby brown tubes poured from the hole. The cylinders clattered as they struck the wooden deck. Distracted from his fretting William ordered, "What is that? Let me see."

The dark-skinned man picked up several of the objects and replied in broken English, "Musket cartridges, senhor."

William's stomach dropped as if the ship had fallen from the crest of a ninety-foot swell. He ran to the sack, tearing back more of the material. Neatly hidden inside the sack of beans was another, smaller bag of cartridges.

Aghast, William ran over the meaning of this unexpected find. If unauthorized trading meant the confiscation of a ship and imprisonment, arms dealing meant death. In fact, if he were suspected of trading with the French, there would not be the formality of a trial; he would hang from a yardarm in less than an hour. William attempted to move the sack, but what should not have weighed more than fifty pounds was at least double that.

At that moment the whiz of a single cannon-shot sailed overhead, followed by the bang of the gun. William's head snapped up in time to see the white plume drifting from the warship. The obvious question of who had planted this contraband evaporated like the fumes. The signal to heave-to had been given; the Royal Marines were going to board.

"Shall I back the sails, senhor?"

William was frantic with worry. How would he hide the damaged sack? Surely they would see it right by the landing. He could not throw it overboard, for the navy vessel was already too close, and they would surely see this and search everything. William was not so naive as to believe there was but *one* contraband container.

The question came again. "Do we comply, Captain?"

"No!" William shouted to the hands who were standing by to take the motion off the ship. "Stand by to come about!" he commanded. "All hands! Prepare to lay her on the starboard tack!"

Confused, the hands did not move. Could this crazy American think to run out from under the British guns?

He yelled his orders again. This time the men complied, and the helmsman spun the wheel.

Another puff of smoke showed the English were tiring of the delay: *stop or be sunk* was the message.

The second shot tore right through the rigging of the main topsail. Bursting lines and stays, the released tension flung a topman flying, barely missing the deck in his descent.

Seconds later the frantic sailor bobbed up from the cold depths and began to cry for help. One of the men scurried to throw out a lifeline. The *Julia*, caught in mid-maneuver between backing the sails and clapping onto the opposite tack, drifted aimlessly. She was running down on the warship as if intentionally trying to ram.

"Heave-to! Back the main!" William cried, sensing that just a minute more remained before total destruction.

For an instant the starboard side was obscured from the British view, shielded by the mounds of cargo. "Hurry!" William motioned to three of the sailors. "Throw this sack overboard!"

The men were again baffled. Why would the Yankee want to jettison a ripped but otherwise perfectly sound bit of cargo? William lifted the sack partly by himself, and then the crewmen likewise spotted the dribbled cartridges. They realized the imminent danger, and a second later the incriminating container of gunpowder and beans splashed over the side and was on its way to the bottom.

"You men say nothing of this," William ordered.

Several of the crew translated his words into mumbled Portuguese; all of them nodded.

Minutes later the *H.M.S. Bethesda* pulled alongside. Grappling hooks wedded the two vessels together as the muzzles of the British guns rested directly against the *Feliciatas Julia*.

A haughty, red-coated marine lieutenant boarded with several others. "Who's in charge here?" he queried imperiously.

William stepped forward and stated with more self-assurance than he felt, "I'm in charge, Lieutenant."

"Let me see your papers," the officer barked, even though William was holding them in his outstretched hand. The lieutenant snatched them away. "And where are you bound?"

The most dreaded of all questions, William thought. How could he answer, not knowing if his answer would release the tension or put a noose around his neck. "Corunna," he blurted. "With supplies to be distributed to Wellington's armies."

"Aren't you American?"

"Correct. William Summerset is my name."

"I didn't ask for your name, you bleedin' Yankee fleabag. And you look nervous too," the man said, nudging William's leg with the toe of his shiny boot. "What 'ave you got to be nervous about, I wonder?"

While this exchange was proceeding, another figure crossed from the *Bethesda,* this man dressed in the uniform of a Royal Navy officer. William hardly looked up, but a glance out of the corner of his eye brought his head up sharply. It could not be, he thought. Was it truly Thomas Burton, once his best friend, whom William had last seen being captured by the French six years before?

Suddenly all implications of the revelation struck him: Thomas might not be glad to see him. William suspected that Thomas believed William had deserted him and was convinced the Suttons *were* traitors. In fact, when Thomas recognized

William Sutton hiding inside William Summerset, he might be pleased to arrest him. Dread washed over William.

Thomas was examining the cargo ship as he boarded. Not even regarding William, he took the papers from the first lieutenant of the Royal Marines.

"Summerset 'ere says 'e's 'eaded for Corunna with a load of food for Wellington's troops."

Thomas looked over the papers. "And is this true, Mister Summer . . ." He had merely begun to speak when his eyes met William's. Thomas gasped, then covered up his surprise by clearing his throat. Putting on a steely expression, he questioned, "What is your name?"

William remained hopeful, answering, "William Summerset, sir."

"And you have official business with His Majesty's Army?"

"I do, sir," William replied formally. "To deliver these food stores."

His eyes darting surreptitiously around while speaking, William tried to watch everything at once as others in the boarding party poked and prodded sacks and crates.

Thomas perused him seriously. "Take me to

your private quarters, Mr. Summerset. Lieutenant Sloan seems to think you are not what you seem."

So this was to be the end of him. Thomas must be consumed with hate. He was certain Thomas wished to have it out in private before turning him over to the marines as a prisoner. "Certainly, Captain," William managed to say.

The two men made their way back to the owner's quarters.

Thomas halted when he realized he was being followed. "Lieutenant Sloan," he shouted. "Where are you going?"

The marine officer stopped in his tracks. "Accompanying you, sir. To guard Mister Summerset, sir."

Thomas looked William up and down before stating, "Does this look like a dangerous man to you, Lieutenant? I hardly think an American who would deliver food to Wellington's army could be a threat." Thomas faced William where Sloan could not see and raised an eyebrow.

"No, sir, but . . ." Sloan argued.

Thomas barked, "Do you have difficulty understanding my order, Lieutenant Sloan?"

Sloan fumbled to attention. "No, sir."

"Wellington's army does not concern you, so stand down! In fact, have your men cease what they are doing. Remain on watch, but take no more action."

Neither Thomas nor William waited for the clumsy reply before entering the cabin. Once inside, with the door shut behind them, both men gazed at one another in the grip of deep emotion.

A burning sensation in his chest made his heart glow and his scalp lift and William surged forward. He and Thomas embraced, without saying a word. "I thought I'd never see you again."

Thomas patted William's back as they stepped apart. "For a long time I was angry. I named you coward and a hundred ugly things."

He was interrupted when William defended himself. "But I couldn't turn around, you see! The rudder was jammed—"

Thomas cut him off. "I know, I know. I found out after I returned to England in a prisoner exchange." His eyes met William's with concern. "Then I heard that your family had been run out of England because of Albert. Some trumped-up nonsense about your being traitors."

"Yes," William replied, rubbing his forehead at the memory.

"I knew better. Remember that your nemesis, Sea Lord Malcolm, is also the one who took Miss

McReady away from me. I knew him to be treacherous. But enough history. You married Dora! Congratulations! And how is your brother?"

"He is well. With his wife, Angelique, and three children, they live several houses away from us in Baltimore."

"And your grandfather and mother?"

"My mother has passed on. My ship commemorates her."

Thomas nodded sadly, rolling his head back. "So *Feliciatas Julia*."

"And Grandfather is finding renewed life in American politics." William's speech was abbreviated by another thought. "Thomas! No war! And we might have met as enemies!"

"Amen to avoiding that tragedy!" Thomas said with a smile.

William gripped Thomas's forearm. "I will see you soon in Baltimore, I hope." William wanted to mention his boy, Billy, but a wave of guilt strangled him. Was it because he was lying to his friend about their cargo, or was it to do with Michelle Braganza?

This mental conflict was unperceived by Thomas, who continued, "William, despite using a false identity, you must be careful when trading on the Spanish coast, even with the army. Six years is a long time, but the memories possessed by those who have wronged you are longer yet and they fear the truth. There may be a price on your head, and no amount of money is worth losing your life over."

The statement sank deep into the sea of William's mind. In it he swam to keep from sinking, but had no energy left for words. A parting hug and before William realized what had happened, Thomas had rounded up his men and bid safe journey to the ship.

As the *Bethesda* departed, William felt as if lost at sea: tossed in the wake and floating adrift. Reunited with Thomas and finding his comrade as truehearted as ever, William had allowed the separation of deception to remain.

At last, thinking of the joy he experienced at learning that his good friend from childhood lived, William allowed warmth to creep back into his lips again. The thought made him happier than any in a long time, and he vowed to set things right. With a grin as wide as the ocean he ordered, "Set sail, course northeast!"

It was an excited trio that left the Sutton household for their various objectives: Grandfather to see his banker and then on to confer with Assistant Vicar Sheffield, Angelique toward the market in search of goats and other provisions, and Dora, a determined set to her jaw, off to locate wet nurses.

"Dora," Angelique had said, "I will see to the livestock and clothing for your foundlings, but you must see to the nurses for the infants. You will please to remember, there must be one nurse for every three childrens."

Dora wondered where she could possibly find a single wet nurse, let alone the several she was certain would be needed.

While strolling in the market past the vendors hawking their wares, Dora spotted Charlene Dillard. Mrs. Dillard, a member of the Episcopal congregation, had recently employed a wet nurse for her infant twin boys.

Thinking it Divine Providence, Dora approached Mrs. Dillard in hopes of gleaning information from her.

"Good morning, Mrs. Dillard." Dora offered the greeting cautiously.

"Mmm. Yes. I suppose it is. How are you, Dora?"

"I am well, thank you. And your children? They are faring . . . ?"

Mrs. Dillard, suspicious of Dora's hesitation,

answered abruptly, "We are all fine, Dora. Now, did you have a purpose in mind for this idle chitchat or was there something else? I have much to do in town today."

Dora had not expected to have to address the issue bluntly. She had expected to have time to sound out Charlene Dillard as to the notion. That device destroyed, Dora stammered her reply. "Umm, yes. I mean . . . Charlene, you see, I've spoken with Vicar Sheffield about the fate of colored infants. The unwanted babies of the Baltimore slave market. I believe it a tragedy that they should be left to die. The vicar is allowing me the use of the vacant parsonage so I can begin to take them in. I was hoping, Charlene, that you could tell me how to obtain a wet nurse, or several, actually."

Charlene Dillard heaved an irritated groan and rolled her eyes heavenward before replying. "Why, Dora Sutton! A wet nurse is it? For the preservation of cast-off darkies? What can your dear William think of this? Nurses are easy enough to come by; not just any old drooping slave Negress, of course, but an advertisement in *The Sun* for free women of color, like our Mattie, making certain they have references, of course. But that is to contact reputable women for the benefit of white babies, not to have them feed bastard slave brats. What can you be thinking of? And what does William think?" she repeated.

Dora, increasingly humiliated and annoyed at Mrs. Dillard for her unsympathetic view, retorted, "What concern is it of yours what William thinks of it? These are innocent children I'm trying to help."

"Dora," Mrs. Dillard said with a cautionary wag of her finger, "your husband *must* approve of the idea. You would never go against his wishes, surely. To do so would be simply unchristian. You would not be party to rebellion, would you? Everyone knows that rebellion is as the sin of witchcraft. And should you start raising darkies, you would be rearing up the devil's own henchmen. Like beasts they are. Uncivilized animals."

Mrs. Dillard uttered this without a blush in front of her own children's wet nurse, a tall, dignified woman who stood with downcast eyes. Mrs. Dillard continued on self-righteously, "I will pray for you though, that God on high will cleanse you of your selfish and rebellious ways."

Dora's mounting ire got the best of her as she watched Charlene Dillard turn to go. Before Dora knew what was happening, her own voice gave vent to her true feelings. She called after the woman's stiffly rigid back, "Thank you for your opinion, Charlene Dillard! And also for your reverent prayers to *your* god. But don't bother! It's clear you do not serve the same God I do!"

Mrs. Dillard huffed off down the lane. As she did so, with her indignant nose in the air, she had the unfortunate experience of placing her left foot in a fresh pile of horse dung. Her filthy and slippery shoe could no longer hold her weight on the slick cobblestones and her feet came out from under her, landing her in a bigger pile of manure with a squishy thud and a surprised shriek.

Men rushed to help her up, only to be scolded and slapped with her handbag. Meanwhile skirts, hoop, and petticoats worked themselves up over her head, obscuring her face and exposing all else.

Dora allowed herself a chuckle. She muttered that, indeed, the God she served *was* just and fair and had a wonderful sense of humor. As she turned away from the scene, she spotted Charlene's wet nurse with the twins in tow.

Taking her aside, Dora hurriedly whispered, "Episcopal church, old parsonage. I need at least three wet nurses to help me feed the orphaned slave babies. They will be paid."

The woman offered a near-toothless smile and

said, "Lawdy, Missy! I come my own self! I ne'er 'spected I'd be feedin' my own kine! Not after my sweet baby was took wid de fever. Dis yere is a blessin' from heaven, sho'nuff! You don' fret none. We be dere, yes'm, we be dere!"

CHAPTER 7

"Carlos!" William had to restrain himself from shouting as he entered the Braganza mansion after a week's absence.

"In here, William," Braganza's lighthearted voice replied. "The signal flags have reported your success. There but remains for you to tell me the details of your voyage."

Fuming, William rounded the corridor into the long study where he had first met Carlos. "You lied to me," William exclaimed before the two men were face-to-face.

Carlos stood, his face etched with concern. Clasping his hands in like a pious cleric and moving from behind the desk, he questioned softly, "William. What do you mean by such hard words?"

William clenched his fists. *He knew . . . knew!*

Carlos was aware of the reason for William's rage, though he played the wounded innocent so well it was difficult to attack the man. Gritting his teeth but responding involuntarily to Braganza's gentling tones, William accused, "You knew there were weapons and ammunition hidden within the food stores, and yet you did not tell me. Why?"

Carlos slipped his arm around William's broad shoulders, ushering him through a passage hidden behind a tapestry and out into the gardens. "William, I am distraught! I must apologize. I thought you understood when I said I had supplies for the guerrilla fighters that it meant *all* types of supplies. Surely this was clear enough?"

"One of the sacks of beans broke open minutes before I was stopped by a British frigate. I had to scramble to rid the ship of the evidence, while musket cartridges poured over the deck. I could have been shot, had they found out!"

Carlos Braganza made a deprecating gesture as if to say, it could not be as bad as that.

"My paperwork said nothing of munitions and weapons. Had they been found, my entire ship would have been confiscated and myself tried for treason and executed on the spot."

His voice quavering with emotion, Carlos spoke.

"I am sorry, I would never . . ." He crossed himself with pious deliberation. "As God is my witness, I would never have sent you into harm."

William cut him off. "Carlos, if we are to continue doing business together, you must be honest with me in the future."

Lowering his head at the offensive words, Braganza resembled a bull preparing to charge. "Carlos dishonest? This is a strong statement for someone who was promised double wages for a simple job he contracted to perform! Perhaps you would no longer like to do business with me then, eh?"

William thought rapidly of his ambition for the American Coastal Shipping Company. Carlos could make or break his success, so William backed down. "I apologize. I was concerned for the safety of my ship and myself."

"Apology accepted," Braganza said, his attitude changing as suddenly as a burst of sunlight breaking through the clouds after a rainstorm. "It was a successful mission . . . no harm done . . . and you have earned a pretty fortune in gold. We have that to be thankful for. Leave Senhor Fussel with me when you return to America, and we will plan a bountiful partnership."

The sound of footsteps on gravel caught his

attention. Both men turned as Michelle appeared in a long white cotton dress. Her shoulders were bare, and her skin a golden brown. A scarf of brilliant turquoise was tied around her waist and draped across one hip.

"Oh, Michelle!" Carlos cried sweetly. "See who has returned?"

"And he is truly welcome! Hello, dear William." Running to William's side, Michelle stood on tiptoe, leaned toward William's cheek, and kissed him.

Once again in awe of her exotic beauty, William eyed her up and down. He tried to return a proper, courteous salutation, but could hardly make the words come out.

The tantalizing aromas of citrus and flowers aroused his senses. "Yes, Michelle . . . Hello."

She remained close to him. Uneasy, William slid back a step, and she moved closer. "How is your poor head?" Michelle asked, caressing his forehead where the knot had been.

William's body became hot, and he froze where he stood, though he could not look her in the face.

"Let me see." She ran her fingers down his cheek, tugging his chin to hers.

His eyes darted toward the ivy-covered walls, the bubbling fountain, and the sky, but once they locked with hers he could not turn away. Michelle's glossy hazel eyes hypnotized him, while speaking to his deepest desires. Taking her hand from his face, William said, "It's fine, really. Much better, thank you." With a groan that he fumbled into a cough, he attempted to change the subject. "Yes, so, Carlos. It was a good voyage indeed."

"Bravo, then, William. I knew it would be."

"Papa," Michelle cut in, "may we take William to the bullfight tonight?"

"What a grand idea. William," Braganza said, his lips curving, "enough talk of business. You must go and experience Portugal as it was meant to be lived."

Exhausted from the journey, William wanted to say no, but again could not refuse the persuasive Carlos Braganza.

Michelle, advancing another step, ran her hand down William's strong chest. "Wonderful, William. We will have such a time tonight." She kissed him again, this time on the lips, before rushing off.

William stared after her. He thought of his loving Dora back home, then tossed his head as though to clear it from another blow. "Carlos, there is something I must tell you."

Patting William on the back, Braganza insisted, "No more words! Your apology is accepted."

"But I must . . ."

"No, no," Carlos warned. "It is not needed. You make my daughter happy, and you make me happy. Everything is forgotten! But now you must rest, for tonight we celebrate."

Carlos left William standing in the garden with the word *wife* on the tip of his tongue. Perhaps the mood was too good to upset right then, he thought, and so, for the sake of business, the truth would have to wait until later.

In less than a week Dora and Angelique gathered livestock, feed for the goats and chickens, and an astonishing eight wet nurses, while four others were turned away but asked to keep in contact. The Negro women sang hymns as they organized the shelves in the pantry and the kitchen cupboards with the accumulated supplies. Billy and Cyrus stacked crates and boxes and loaded bins with cornmeal and flour.

The rooms in the former parsonage were converted to nurseries with donated bedding and empty soapboxes to be used for cradles. Two women were assigned to each of the four rooms. Each had a bed and a drawer of her own, and each took turns caring for and milking the goats to provide milk for the older babies.

Dora fretted that her carefully budgeted funds barely provided enough salary for three nurses to be paid. But in the end it was not an issue, since each of the eight said they were content with room and board and felt privileged to offer life-sustaining nourishment to the little ones.

At eight o'clock the following morning Angelique bustled in, flushed with excitement, carrying two squawking foundlings, one tucked into the crook of each arm.

By noon of the same day the bell at the parsonage door had jangled five times with seven more infants being left for care and one more offer of help. A bashful German baker and his forthright and outspoken wife said they had "heard about Gott's work being done and would supply two-day-old bread for free. That would a help be, yah?"

"Yah, yes!" Dora said with delight.

News of the "foundling house" spread quickly through the colored part of town, through the market, and down on the docks where slaves were being bought, sold, and traded.

Grandfather Sutton brought Billy and Dora's

dinner by at half-past four in the afternoon and found Dora and the others hurrying about among the ten babies.

By nine at night, Dora left exhausted, smelling like regurgitated milk and appearing more than a little disheveled. And radiant.

She informed the nurses she would return by seven the next morning and bid them good night.

Dora rose at 5:30 A.M. the next morning after a restorative and dreamless night's sleep. She bathed and dressed then breakfasted alone.

Billy joined her at 6:30, already clad and asking if he could accompany her to the orphanage for the day.

"I'd like to see the babies, Mother. I'll bet I could help with the feedings."

Dora debated the wisdom of having an active six-year-old boy in a house of women and children, but in the end she gave in. Perhaps he could keep some of them entertained with his antics.

They arrived at the parsonage several minutes before seven, and it was buzzing with activity. Dora went straight to Opal, the self-appointed head nurse, and a large, good-natured woman whose laugh shook her all over and came from way down inside her ample belly. She had twinkling hazel eyes that sparkled when she talked and lips that parted to reveal two rows of perfect teeth.

When Dora asked for a report of the last night's activity, Opal's response was brief. "Oh, Miz Sutton. Not a one a us slept a wink, but these chillins is well-fed this mawnin'." She chortled at this and winked at Billy, who laughed right back at her.

"Gracious," Dora replied. "I never thought! I should have stayed myself. I'm so sorry."

"No need to be sorry, honey lamb. We's happy to do it. Dem babies is like to our own. We took turns singin' an' tellin' how Jesus loves 'em and feeds 'em jus' like the lilies o' the field an' how He loves the children the bes' in the whole wide worl'."

Billy had slipped from behind his mother's skirt and gone exploring through the house, peering into each of the four nursery rooms and watching the older babies suckle goat's milk from twisted rags. Babies were being bathed and changed, and then one of the nurses asked Billy to fetch a bucket of water from the pump outside. He called over his shoulder to his mother, and out he went.

He had no sooner closed the door than he tripped over a bundle on the step. He was taken aback when the thing bleated pitifully at the disturbance.

Peeling back the dirty rags revealed the tiniest of tiny babies. A scrawled note simply gave her name: Alliebama. Allie, as Billy would call her, locked eyes with him and smiled. She looked to be all gums and eyes.

He scooped her up and hurried back inside with his precious parcel.

Allie was hungry but cried and fussed whenever Billy left her sight, so Billy was immediately employed in helping to change her and feed her, and when the time was right and Allie's eyes grew leaden, Billy sat in a rocking chair and rocked the infant girl to sleep.

From then on, Allie was Billy's special charge, and he took extra care to see she had everything she needed.

At one week out of Lisbon and homeward bound, gale-force winds tore at the triple-reefed sails of the *Julia,* and she labored to climb every mountain of a swell. Once atop each massive wave, the vessel swooped downward, plunging into the trough like a knife blade.

Clippers, because of their narrow beam, were superb at speed but dangerous to control in squalls. It took constant attention to the set of the sails and four men at the wheel to keep her from broaching and capsizing.

The constant thrashing had become monotonous and devastating to physical well-being and the ship's existence. The galley fires had been extinguished for safety, and there had been no hot food for forty-eight hours. The crew members were tired and sullen.

In the dim light of William's cabin he swayed in his hammock listening to planks creaking, and waves crashing against the side of the boat, and the unrelenting rattle of the chain pump, bringing water out of the bilge.

In spite of the real and present danger to life and limb, William could not escape his own thoughts. It seemed Michelle was like the wind. Thoughts of her sent squalls pounding through his mind like the tempest that drove his vessel. When the barometer first fell and the wind rose, it felt exciting and adventurous, much like the mesmerizing Miss Braganza. But was there danger ahead amid uncontrolled forces?

In contrast, he thought of Dora as calm seas.

She was stable and as predictable as a fair, unchanging, three-knot breeze: reliable, not exotic; comforting, not thrilling.

Which was better for a man who wanted to rule the world from an empire of clipper ships?

Like the confused seas that pummeled the *Julia* from every direction, William's musing was battered between desire and guilt.

A knock at the door roused him from his jostled daydreams. "Sir, we have spotted a drifting longboat."

William swung from his hanging bed, pausing to button on a slicker and tie the strings of a floppy brimmed hat under his chin before scurrying on deck. Nightmares of his father's death in a similarly raging sea clouded his mind. "Give me the glass," he told Captain Drake, "and steer for the spot."

The telescope resolved a speck into a recognizable shape. Several hundred yards away bobbed a longboat; a mere splinter of wood in the deluge. It appeared and disappeared at the whim of the storm. As the *Julia* drew closer, William could see the unmoving form of a lone man huddled in the stern.

Heaving-to in such a tempest was a huge menace to the clipper and her crew. A vagrant gust might lay her on her beam ends and be their death. What if the figure were a corpse? Was it worth the risk? Slicing through the waves at over fifteen knots, the clipper had already closed half the distance. Once astern, the drifting survivor would certainly be lost forever. There could be no turning back amid such a storm.

William thought of his father, who had been shipwrecked and had died in the sea when William and Albert were but babies. "Back the sails. Bring us up to windward. Prepare to heave the lifelines."

It would be a difficult extraction at best, to rescue a man from angry seas without crushing him under the ship in the rolling swells. There would be perhaps a minute's chance and then irretrievable loss.

The man was alive. The single occupant of the lifeboat crouched but waved arms overhead, frantic that they not sail past.

William himself stood at the rail with a weighted messenger line. Four others were ahead of him along *Julia*'s portside. There was no method of braking the clipper that would take the momentum off of her, and Captain Drake would have to do a dangerously delicate bit of steering to lay them near enough alongside without crushing the longboat.

The first rope was thrown too soon. It fell uselessly into the waves before the boat was within reach. The second and third sailors, hoping to avoid that error, made the toss too late, after the longboat had drifted too far astern.

The fourth rope sailed across the craft from gunnel to gunnel. The survivor lunged for it, but it yanked out of reach as *Julia* wallowed in an unexpected swell.

Only William stood between the man and his death. Though William could not hear the panicked screams, he could see the agonized appeal on the man's face.

The next toss was perfectly directed and timed. The weighted end sailed over the castaway's head and into his eagerly grasping fingers.

Julia was ripped up by another swell. The man was yanked from his craft and hammered into the clipper's side. The thud of his body could be heard despite the noisy elements of nature. Had it knocked him loose into the depths?

William leaned over the side and shouted; "Hold on, man!" The figure remained, though his feet dangled in the spume, and he could not haul himself up. "To me!" William yelled to the other sailors. "Grab hold and heave!"

The man was lifted from the water just as the swell turned loose of the clipper. *Julia*'s stern crashed down on the longboat, smashing it into splinters and dunking the poor soul again. "Hang on, I say!"

As the vessel lurched again, so too did William and the crew. The castaway dangled half dead, banging against the side. Minutes later, he was lifted from the seas to the security of William's ship. Collapsed on the deck, he panted the words, "Thank . . . you . . . Saved my life."

Stripped of his sodden clothing, wrapped in blankets and plied with restoratives until his teeth stopped chattering, the rescued castaway was finally able to answer questions.

"What ship?" William wanted to know. "Lost in the storm?"

With an apprehensive face, the man asked William, "Are you English?"

"Yes, but I left Britain six years ago. I assure you, you are safe with us. Who are you, and how did you come to be lost at sea?"

"Able Seaman Warren," the sailor replied, knuckling his forehead. "My ship, *Flora* out of Nantucket, was attacked by a British frigate when we refused to heave-to for boarding. It happened as this squall blew up. One broadside holed us below the waterline, and another tangled main and mizzen-masts over the side and drug us athwart the waves. I cut a longboat free as the ship was going down! I am the only one I know of who survived."

"Attacked! What is this nonsense you speak? England has repealed the Orders in Council. There will be no war with America."

Warren shook his head. "No sir, you're mistaken. President Madison declared war."

A wave of dread hammered William as cold as the spray from the sea. He leaned hard against a rail. Reality soaked and chilled him to the core. The difference between war and no war was the time it took messages to cross the Atlantic. A cursed delay had changed everything!

"Is there no turning America back from war?" William blurted, though he did not expect this sailor to have an answer.

"I do not believe so, sir, for America seized several British vessels in harbor after the word came from Congress. Once the British fleet commander heard it, the Royal Navy responded speedily enough. There's no turning back. War is unavoidable."

"No one is listening!" Albert exclaimed to Secretary Monroe. "The British have attacked and seized Mackinaw, and General Hull has surrendered Detroit with barely so much as a shot being fired, and yet the politicians say, 'It is far out west. It does not affect us here!' *Sacré bleu!* What will affect them then? When the British Admiral Cochrane sails up the Potomac and sticks his cannon in their . . ."

"Calm yourself, Albert," Monroe soothed. "You are right, but you go too far. Besides, you don't seriously expect the British to attack Washington? Who wants this mudhole anyway? But we must be better prepared, for they will hit Boston or New York or even Baltimore."

"That is precisely my point," Albert said. "I cannot stay here arguing whether General X is taking too much horse feed from General Y's horses while neither of them commands enough men to raise a flag! And the way everyone prates of his own state without regard to the whole country. *Diable!* Then me, also! I wish to go to see to the defense of my home: Baltimore."

Monroe assented, but asked, "What about the war at sea? Will American Coastal Shipping Company be interested in privateering ventures?"

"Privateering? Officially sanctioned piracy?"

Laughing, Monroe concurred, "If you like. But we know the British will try to hurt our trade with a blockade. I say, let's hurt them right back. Make our navy seem bigger; spread their forces over a wider area; capture *their* merchantmen on the high seas; make their men of business see reason. The president supports this idea."

More calmly Albert said, "I see what you mean. Let me send a message to my grandfather in Baltimore and consider what can be arranged."

"Good," Monroe acknowledged. "And then please report back to me."

When the *Julia* dropped anchor by night in Baltimore Harbor all seemed quiet, deathly quiet. The water was the smoothest it had been the entire voyage. The breeze that succeeded the Atlantic gale diminished to barely a whisper that wafted the clipper home, then died away. The air, unpleasant with the stickiness of summer, was heated further by a blazing bonfire near the docks. Besides the conflagration, hundreds of torches circled and wove about like a swarm of giant fireflies.

Instead of the joyful relief of making landfall

after peril, fear struck William like a familiar ax that glances off a hard knot of wood to strike the wielder; it felt treacherous, like a betrayal.

War! he thought. Had it begun? Had he arrived on the heels of a British invasion and was a battle already under way?

"I don't like the look of this," Captain Drake muttered. "I see no Royal Navy ships, but they might have slipped a party overland."

Likewise wary, William almost ordered Drake to put to sea again, in fact, would have if there had been any wind. "Stay here," he commanded. "Keep a close watch. Arm the men and line both rails so no one slips up on you. Don't let anyone board unless they give you the watchword." William thought a moment. "Which is *Portugal*. Even if you see me in the boat, don't let it come near unless I give the word. If anything suspicious happens, or if I'm not back in thirty minutes, weigh anchor and tow her out to midchannel."

Twelve combat-worthy sailors, one of whom was the fully recovered Curtis Warren, armed with pistols and cutlasses, rowed William ashore in a longboat. Leaving two to guard the launch, William gathered the others around him and swarmed briskly up the gangway.

As he approached the storm of lights, the waving torches resolved into a shouting, gesturing mob, whose antics and furious voices resembled more of a war dance of red Indians than a battlefield. The piercing pungency of burning pitch and tar aroused William's fighting instincts. His heart beat faster, and he noticed himself swell inches taller as he flexed his muscles and gathered himself for conflict.

Out of the crowd came a familiar voice. "William!"

Turning, William could at first just spot a hand waving to him from the middle of a mass of swarming bodies. Then, like a bar of slippery soap being squeezed out of a hand, his brother Albert was catapulted out of the crowd.

"William!"

"Albert, what is happening here?"

"America has declared war."

"I know! But what is this midnight mob? And how did you know I was here?"

"There is a boy who works for Captain Shraider. He was posted to notify us if any of the proposed League's vessels should return. He gave the word that the *Julia* had been seen in the offing at sunset."

"League? What league? Who is Shraider? Albert, tell me what is going on."

"Another commercial vessel was attacked by a British man-of-war. After declaring war, America has done nothing to back its declaration. The people of Baltimore want to fight! This demonstration is the result. But come with me. We must hurry as I have important news from Washington and am just back tonight myself."

William had no time for further inquiry before he was jerked by the arm and guided past the mob, down an alleyway. His bodyguard cleared the way ahead, tossing drunkards and torch-waving slogan shouters out of their path. "Where are we going?"

"To an important meeting."

William dragged his feet. "No, wait. I've barely stepped on home soil. I'm not going to any meeting with a bunch of shouting rowdies who found their courage in a tavern and are threats to barrels of tar! They will run at the first sight of a red uniform or a raised musket." He began to turn around.

Albert grasped his brother's shoulder. "William, it's not what you think. You must come. If something is not done, there will be no home soil."

The threat sunk into William's tired mind. "What is the subject of this urgent council then?"

"Privateering," Albert replied seriously, pausing outside a nondescript door in the side of a tavern.

Privateering, William pondered. *Legalized piracy. Attacking British merchant ships. Perhaps there is money to be made in this war.* "All right," he said. "But I have to give some orders first. Addressing *Julia*'s crewmen, he called, "Return to the ship and keep watch. Don't forget to give the signal *Portugal* so you do not get shot!" Then he added, "Warren, I'd like you to come with me."

After climbing three flights of stairs, the trio of men headed down a long hallway before Albert knocked on a crookedly framed door outlined by the light around its edges.

A gruff voice called, "Who is it?"

"Albert."

"Come in," the voice allowed.

Upon entering, William's eyes were immediately drawn to the face of the raspy-voiced speaker. "Hercules Shraider?" William announced with astonishment. "Is that really you?"

"Of course it's me," Shraider, sinewy and squinty-eyed, barked. "Who did you expect? King Bloody George, God rot him?" Shraider grimaced. "Sorry, Randolph. No blasphemy intended."

"Quite all right, Hercules. From you I expect it." This last was spoken by William's grandfather, who emerged from a semicircle of shipping company owners and managers to hug William warmly. "It's good to see you again my boy."

William spoke again to Shraider. "Word came that you were to be executed."

"Aye, but I told them 'no, thank 'ee.'" Shraider raised his brawny, calloused hands. "Strangled my guard with my own two fists, stole a boat, and sailed over six hundred miles of ocean till a Nantucketer plucked me out. More seawater than blood in my bilge by then, eh? Well, told this story a million times already. Let's cut to the chase. Powder and shot and lay 'em by the heels."

Grandfather Sutton interpreted for William. "Shraider here is the strongest voice in favor of privateering. Others are more cautious. Having a peaceful commerce ship seized by the Royal Navy is different from having a pirate vessel blown out of the water."

Shaking his head gravely, William brought Curtis Warren to the fore. "You should listen to what this man has to say."

Warren repeated the tale of his ship's destruction at the hands of the British.

"There, you see?" Shraider said vehemently.

"No reason to hold back. It's all-out war, ain't it? Let the League of Deliverance from British tyranny fire the first shots!"

"There is reason for caution," a portly German merchant named Gestenberg objected. "Unless the government in Vashington sanctions us, ve may all as pirates be hanged. Unt ve may not be zo lucky as Captain Shraider."

Albert interjected, "So you will outfit commerce raiders if President Madison and the Congress will support you?"

There was a rumble of agreement in the room.

"Then it is settled," Albert said, removing a sheaf of papers from the bosom of his jacket. "Congress may continue to debate about invading Canada and such, but here are duly signed and sealed letters of marque, awaiting simply the addition of the ships' names and the signatures of the owners. Each proclaims the bearer to be duly authorized to carry out attacks on the enemies of the United States and insists that the same bearer be treated as a prisoner of war, should he be captured."

"Hurrah!" Shraider rasped. "How pieces of paper can move men off their backsides." He hoisted a tankard of ale. "Here's to successful cruises and a speedy conclusion to the Second War of Independence." He winked at William. "But not too speedy, eh?"

After the toast was drank, Grandfather Sutton queried, "And what of outfitting of these ships? Where and with what shall we arm them?"

"The president's directive also allows us to purchase weaponry from federal arsenals and foundries and the money used to pay the regulars and militiamen who fight the land battles."

William confidently added, "And I know a man who is at present arming the Spanish guerrilla fighters. His help will make resupplying our ships possible even across the Atlantic."

"Braganza," Grandfather noted.

"The same," William said with assurance. "He will have no problems dealing with us. Our company representative is already there."

While the rest of the occupants of the sweaty-hot room fell to discussing cannon and shot, strategy and tactics, and likely places of ambush, William did some fast calculations of his own. What a glorious opportunity to make money when capturing enemy vessels and selling off their goods. The way for the American Coastal Shipping Company to come out on top would be to set out as the first privateer, hammer a few British vessels, and sell off their cargoes to expand this private war. Then an unpleasant thought struck him. What would have happened to William in his last encounter with a Royal Navy ship if it had not been for Thomas Burton? A friend who risked his life for him. What would happen should William come upon Thomas once more, this time sailing as a privateer? Both would have to do their duty. William banished the fearsome anticipation from his mind.

Grandfather Sutton ventured to the window, yanking back the curtains. An orange glow from the mob-scene torches flooded the room. "America is a vessel adrift, gentlemen. The smooth seas of true independence cannot be reached without crossing the reef of war. It is regrettable and tragic, but inescapable. And this war, which was brought on by issues at sea, must be settled at sea." He pointed to the weaving lights that danced on the darkness like lighted ships bobbing on the waves. "These angry patriots will sober up and stagger home. Their screams will do nothing to win the war. We must pledge our allegiance to America and to the League of Deliverance, for it is now up to us."

CHAPTER 8

J ust as Baltimore Harbor had felt too quiet before the riot broke out, William's house after he got away from the meeting of the League of Deliverance seemed unnaturally silent as well. He stepped into the entry to reclaim the calming effect that the dwelling had always possessed for him at previous homecomings: the aroma of spiced potpourri; the satisfying smell of wax from the highly polished furniture; Dora's homey, lavender-water-based perfume.

He let out a sigh. "It's good to be back," he said, glancing around the dim but glistening parlor. Nothing had changed in the months he was away, he thought. Comforted by the tall clock ticking away at the foot of the stairs, William set down his bags. Light on his feet, he flew up the stairs to check on little Billy.

The door creaked ever so slightly. Pale light from the oil-fired streetlamp flickered into the room. Billy slept with one leg hanging over the bed and the other resting on the windowsill. His hair was mussed, and he slept deeply. William kissed him on the forehead. Billy stirred briefly, then groaned, and rolled over to lie facedown on his pillow.

William wanted so badly to wake him, but decided it would be better to save the surprise of his return until morning. He closed the door behind him.

Now for the next and more difficult reunion. What had Dora kept herself occupied with? Had she missed him? He had parted in such haste, such eagerness to be away. Moreover, the greasy feel of a guilty conscience about Michelle Braganza smeared his thoughts of Dora.

William defended himself in his mind. He had not actually done anything with the girl! A whispering voice reminded him that he had never acknowledged he was married, but he brushed that annoying reminder away like a mosquito.

He told himself that the *real* reason he dreaded this encounter was that Dora was so clingy and needy. She would ask a million questions and keep him up with exclamations of anxiety about his travels and the war. She would inquire about the places he went, people he met, she might even make him uncomfortable in relating his meeting with the Braganzas. How dare she make him feel guilty when all he had done was vigorously pursue his profession as a proper man of business should?

Dora's constant agitation over the chasm of their differences had grown tiring to William. The honest part of him knew this was sometimes a way of rationalizing doing what he selfishly wanted. *Though sometimes,* he told himself, *a man is driven by his loved ones to do the things they are most afraid of him doing. First they plant a seed of worry. Then as it grows to obsession, they entertain the thought as if it were true; treat it as reality. The constant agitation becomes emotional punishment for sins not yet committed. And what man would stand for certain punishment regardless of guilt?*

He was constantly being forced to reassure Dora, to deny her worries and accusations. It was hardening his heart and making him good with denial. *I know what to expect, what she will ask of me, and what I will say to make her feel at ease. But I will not fret over this, for my thoughts have remained merely thoughts and not actions.* Relief washed through him as he turned the knob.

"Dora," he whispered, "are you awake?"

"No," she responded in a muzzy, sleep-fuddled voice. "But you are home, and I am content."

"Yes," he acknowledged, smiling in the night, moving to comfort her. He kissed her on the cheek. "I missed you."

"I missed you too." She rolled away. "I'm sorry, William. I'm too tired to talk. I must get up early tomorrow. There is much work."

William slipped off his clothes. Why did she not jump from bed to embrace him? Why did she not ask him the probing questions? Was she truly so very tired that his long-awaited return could not even wake her from sleep? "Dora, is everything all right?"

She rubbed her eyes, more awake, or at least trying. "Yes, everything is fine, William. Was it a good voyage?"

"It was. A profitable voyage. I met with my old friend Thomas Burton. He saved my life when I ran supplies to the Spanish guerrilla fighters. We earned double the usual fee in gold sovereigns." He waited for her to rise and share in his excitement, but she did not. Was this her way of punishing him

for leaving? If it was, how could she not understand that business was the way it was? He must
leave and travel and be exposed to danger. That
was what the Suttons did.

"That's wonderful . . . William," came the yawn-
ing reply with her back turned. "Sorry . . . must
sleep."

Had she somehow sensed with a woman's intu-
ition that this time he had thought of another
woman? Or . . . incredible thought . . . had she been
thinking about another man and was thus indifferent to his arrival? William's conscience plagued him
with worry and wonder. "Good night," he said at
last before tiptoeing to his own room. But she had
already fallen back into sleep.

Over the sounds of chewing, clinking china, rat-
tling silverware, and polite dinner conversation,
Grandfather Sutton cleared his throat and addressed
Dora.

"Tell me, my dear, how were things with the
children today?"

William took no notice at first mention of this
but became increasingly curious as the conversation continued.

During the days since his return from Portugal, Dora had been pleasant, but distant. She expressed happiness at his return, inquired without interest about his plans to mesh American Coastal Shipping with the war effort, and generally left William frustrated and confused.

"Very well, thank you," was Dora's response to what William had perceived as merely polite dinner conversation. "Three children were delivered today. The youngest is just days old and severely undernourished. I do believe, though, that given patience and the continued blessing of Providence, he shall pull through and someday become a strapping young fellow," Dora said enthusiastically.

Billy, not wanting to be left out of this conversation, added his endorsement of Dora's project and his newfound love. "Yes, Grandfather. And Allie . . . she's the one I found outside the church . . . she's the smartest and brightestest . . ."

"Brightest," Dora corrected gently.

"Yes, Mama," Billy said. "And she is too."

William interrupted with an exclamation that demonstrated how clearly he knew he had missed events of tremendous significance. "I'm sorry. I am at a loss." He smiled with false sincerity at his wife. "What's this about children and the church?"

Dora flushed and lost a bit of confidence. "Oh dear. William. I thought surely I . . . or someone . . . had mentioned it to you."

"Mentioned what, Dora? What exactly is it that you may or may not have mentioned to me?" William demanded, growing short-tempered in his quest for information.

"You see there were, uh, there are, I mean the children, you see." Dora drew a ragged breath and glanced at Angelique and Grandfather as she began again, this time without stumbling. "William, you may have noticed that unwanted slave children need attention and decent care. I have taken on this work of charity and begun to organize an orphanage for the abandoned children of Baltimore."

William, who had just taken a swig from his water glass, choked at his wife's revelation, struggled to prevent the water from shooting through his nostrils, and slammed his glass to the table while trying to find his voice and wipe the tears from his now-reddened eyes.

"Dora!" he finally sputtered. "Have you no sense?" This was stated as an opinion and not offered as a question, even a rhetorical one. "You have absolutely no experience with orphans! How can you possibly undertake such a thing?" He laughed in a cruel and demeaning way at his wife who, astonishingly, glared piercingly back at him.

"You can't possibly mean you are going to take on the cares and woes of the entire Negro race in the city of Baltimore?"

At this Grandfather cleared his throat and stared at William. "You will lower your voice and moderate your tone, or you may leave the house, William," he said firmly. "Dora may have been unwise in postponing telling you about her undertaking, but that does not give you license to mock her."

Reducing the level of his sarcasm did not eliminate it completely. "Dora," William said in a more controlled volume, "there are so many. Wouldn't you be happier with something else? Surely we could find you another recreation than the handling of dirty castoffs."

William had failed at his attempt to sound civil, and Dora called him up short. "William, because your ambitions are loftier than the rest of ours does not mean you may appoint yourself judge over who may live and who may die. And I resent your implication that there may be more suitable plans for *my recreation* than the care of children!"

At this, Angelique winked at Dora and made as

if she were discreetly disposing of a piece of gristle into her napkin to hide her approval. This encouragement empowered Dora in her argument and, as things grew increasingly tense, Grandfather excused himself from the table and encouraged the others to do the same. It was not long before William and Dora were left alone in the dining room.

"Do you see what you've done?" William said gruffly. "You've gone and made them uncomfortable. How dare you take such a tone with me! You are like an impudent child, and you have disgraced me in front of my family!"

"Impudent child, is it!" Dora shot back. "I no more disgraced you than you have disgraced yourself, Mister William Sutton! And how dare *you* presume to know what I am about or what interests me! You no more care about me and my interests than you do a dung heap in the middle of the avenue!"

As Dora grew steadily louder in her speech, William attempted to quiet her. "Shhhh, Dora. We can't let our emotions get the better of us."

"Don't you shush me, William. You have your love, and I am not *she!* While you have been about the world catering to your mistress, your precious company, I have been here. Alone. And desperately in need of being needed. Those children, William, are just that: children in need of love and attention and someone to hold them when they cry. I can give that to them, even if you reject it. And God knows I'll never have any others of my own. You won't even come to my bed. And quite honestly, I don't know that I'd have you there. No, William, I have not disgraced your family, and I am not an impudent child. My work will bring honor to this family, and I will become someone of value through it. Impudent child, indeed!"

Hot with the anger of humiliation, William lunged across the table, upsetting glasses and candlesticks. He moved as if to strike her, and she caught his wrist.

Through clenched teeth he growled, "And who are you to speak to me thus? You are merely a woman! You haven't any more rights than the black droppings left by their parents on the stoop of your precious orphanage, except as I say you have."

Trembling, through fiery tears of rage, Dora thrust his wrist back toward him and said, "Has your ambition so corrupted your soul that you can no longer see the hearts of others? I am worthy of love and also capable of giving love. I deserve more than you have given, and if I should find it in the helpless face of another's castoff, what business is it of yours? For so long I have been used and unloved. I have been scarcely more than a coatrack to you, and now I have found what makes my heart quicken. I feel human again, William. Where is the harm in that? Is it wrong to offer hope to others? Is it offensive to you that I should find self-worth in caring about something as much as you care about your work? Or is it that you cannot stand to think of me as an individual with ambitions of my own?"

Relaxing his jaw, William sat back with a sigh as Dora let his wrist slip through her palm. "But Dora, let's be reasonable. I'm sorry I was harsh, but you must see things from my point of view. Your involvement with these . . . orphans cannot be good for business. There are still those who fail to understand the issues surrounding slavery. What will people say . . . people of our class in society . . . if they learn of your preoccupation with slave children?"

Dora, once again angry, replied, "Even now in your apology you make this about your own selfish interests. When will you realize that *you* are the impudent child here? You accused me, but you put on airs like a spoiled brat who cannot get the others to play by his rules. I will say this once and once only, William, I am an adult. I happen to be married to you. You are gone most of the time and happy to be so. This commitment gives me purpose. It is what I will for my life in your absence, and I will have it. If you are finished lecturing this child, then I will find my way to bed. Should you also find yourself there then so be it, but I will not discuss this matter further. Is that clear?"

William, pale with the effects of his wife's tongue-lashing, turned his head and traced the lines on the lace tablecloth with his finger while carelessly dismissing her with a brush of his other hand.

She nodded her assent and said, "Good night then, William." And she left him to his miserable musings with a rustle of fine silk and a slam of the door.

If reports of the war in the autumn of 1812 were divided into equal parts of good news and bad news, then it was equally true that the bad news concerned the land battles and the good the conflict at sea.

An American invasion force assembled to make

a lightning thrust into Canada was intercepted and routed near Niagara, almost before the expedition had begun. There were charges and countercharges about who was supposed to provide support, make diversions, protect supply lines from Indian raids, and so forth. In actual fact, *all* of the higher-ranking commanders were inept, and their militiamen troops were poorly trained and apt to flee at the first sign of danger.

Fortunately for the life of the Second War of Independence, the battles on the ocean had a much different outcome.

British ships of the line were committed to containing Napoleon in Europe. Consequently, British blockade and patrol duty off the coast of America fell to British frigates rather than larger warships. The United States had nothing to match the firepower of a vessel like Nelson's *Victory,* but in frigate-to-frigate battles, she held her own and even triumphed.

On the nineteenth of August, the *U.S.S. Constitution,* after having captured three British merchantmen, engaged, defeated, and sank His Majesty's ship *Guerriere.* In mid-October, while William Sutton worked twenty-hour days seeing to the refitting of *Julia* as a raiding vessel, the

U.S.S. Wasp captured the English brig *Frolic,* while sustaining less than a quarter of the amount of casualties.

A week later, the American frigate *United States* fought, dismasted, and captured the British ship *Macedonian.* The English frigate was towed into New York Harbor, and valued at two hundred thousand dollars, which sum was apportioned to the crewmen of the *United States.*

"Two hundred thousand!" William said with a whistle as he read over the dispatch Albert handed him. "Our fortune is made! If we can put to sea before the prizes are snapped up!"

Dryly, Albert observed, "I think there is no concern on that score! This war shows no sign of going away soon. There will be plenty of time for you to play your part."

William, noting the change from the plural pronoun he had used to the singular spoken by his brother, asked about the difference. "Aren't you going to join me? Treasure ships sailing home from Jamaica. Indiamen caught beating up the coast of Africa. You in *Heart of Allegiance* and me in *Julia.* We can seize our share and be fabulously wealthy."

"It is not for me, *mon frere,*" Albert corrected. "You forget, I am not the willing sailor. Besides, my heart and my duty are here. I have promised Angelique and Secretary Monroe that I will under-take the defensive plan of Baltimore."

"Defense!" William snorted. "Who ever won a war by defense?"

"Sometimes," Albert replied, "it is just as important to arrange that one does not *lose* a war."

William looked glum, then shook it off. "All right, then, we'll say no more about it. But I am going to take *Allegiance* back to sea with me."

After what had been a painfully slow beginning, it finally appeared that the expense of refitting *Julia* as a privateer was worth the expenditure of all the Braganza gold. From where William stood on the dockside, he could see that the conversion of the clipper to an attack vessel was working out. Square ports had been cut in the sides where the cannon could be mounted, and thick oak panels were secured around these to protect the gunners. Work-men scampered alow and aloft, rerigging the braces to take the newly stepped heavier masts.

From being the swiftest thing that skimmed the waves, like a storm petrel racing before a wind, *Julia* had sacrificed a portion of her speed to become instead a bird of prey. The cannonports were virtually invisible, meaning that the enemy would never suspect the clipper had talons until they were fired on. While not being able to match a British ship-of-the-line in firepower, *Julia* could unleash a murderous broadside when the occasion demanded.

The day was peaceful: powder-blue sky overhead, cool breeze, and warm sun. William found himself daydreaming. "I wish Dora could see this." William snorted as if arguing with himself. Dora had no interest in his business, none. He and Dora had become like passing ships. His work carried him into the night, even the wee-morning hours, while she rose early enough that he was unable to wake at that time. It puzzled William to see her so focused on her work, to be pursuing it so passionately. He had thought she had chosen her surprising calling merely to spite him. Could she actually be finding it meaningful, or was she merely displaying a stubborn streak?

"The project," as William mockingly referred to it, was no longer what concerned him. Rather it was more the casting overboard of any concerns for him that she had once felt. *She has hardly said hello, hasn't even come to see my masterpiece.*

He grudgingly admitted to himself that neither had he ventured to see what kind of mother Dora was to the orphaned slave children of Baltimore.

"Mister Sutton," called a deckhand, laboriously dragging a load of capstan bars up the gangplank. The man pointed to the road that led out of the shipyard.

Hopping atop a cable spool, William spied a convoy of sturdy wagons, drawn by equally sturdy Clydesdales, trailering a pair of cannons each. The first wagon rolled past the gangway and then back around, where it stopped under a deck hoist.

A rider in a short coat and crushed-crowned hat climbed awkwardly down. He was a round man with such a pleasant smile that it seemed to be carved permanently on his face, along with the red-veined nose and cheeks that suggested he had a love for drink. "Afternoon."

"Good afternoon, sir."

"Any idea where I can find Mister William Sutton?"

"You already have."

"It is a *pleasure* to meet you. I'm James Shadle, dealer in guns and ammunitions. When Captain Shraider explained in the letter how eager you were to be purchasing guns for a privateering vessel, I just had to meet you." The man seized William's hand with his plump fist and pumped it wildly as he talked. "Shraider thinks you've got the stuff to do the country proud."

William bobbed his head with pleasure. "From such a man as the good Captain Shraider, that is high praise indeed. These are for me, I take it."

By then, seventeen wagons had lined up. William looked on with amazement. "Thirty-four guns in all, aye?"

"Yes sir, eight thirty-two-pound carronades. Regular smashers they are; go through a foot of solid oak." Shadle closed his left eyelid, and continued, "If you are within pistol shot that is! Twenty-two eighteen pounders for the main armament, plus two nine-pound long bowchasers for the foredeck, and two more for the stern. Thirty-four in all. And with them the gun carriages to match." Shadle scanned the tall sides of the *Julia*. "More'n three hundred pounds of metal to one broadside makes her the equal of many a British sloop-of-war. She'll slaughter whoever she catches, and by gum, sir, from her lines I say she will call the tune to the dance as well." The man removed his hat in salute, then spoiled the effect by scratching his head with the other hand.

Propelled rudely from his fantasy, William flew into action. "You there, hook up to this hoist, and we shall begin mounting these."

Two by two, the guns were lifted and fitted into place. The *Julia* would pack such fighting fury that William toyed with the idea of renaming her the *Julius Caesar,* conqueror of all he assailed. However, he knew that renaming a ship was bad luck. It crossed his mind that earlier he had allowed her to be renamed for the deception in Spain. But that was different, he told himself. It had been a *ruse de guerre*, meaning "a wartime strategem." He had learned the French phrase from his brother.

CHAPTER 9

———❧———

The fall of 1812 settled almost directly into winter for Baltimore. No one saw the leaves turn colors as war and the threat of invasion loomed increasingly closer to home. Icy winds blew in off the Atlantic, but it was the chill between William and Dora that made the season inexplicably harsh.

Dora and Angelique were busying themselves around the orphanage when Angelique announced, "*Ma cherie*, I have noticed that you are not quite the same of late. I also noticed that your William sees these things too."

"I am sure I don't know what you mean, Angelique. I am the same as ever, just . . . fulfilled. Perhaps that is the word. These babies are God's children, and He has seen fit to use my broken heart to heal the brokenness of these precious ones.

That is certainly more than William has lately offered."

"Tsshah! Dora. So certain you are that your William does not care for you. Perhaps you should soften to him a bit."

Color rose in Dora's throat and cheeks at Angelique's stern admonition.

"Soften! Toward him! Ha! It is not I who am in need of softening! William Sutton has not even been to my bed. All he sees is that ship, and cannons, and racing to get to sea and fight. It's constant talk of privateering . . . and the way he avoids my eyes leaves me empty and cold." Pleading now, Dora said, "Angelique, William sleeps at the shipyard."

Ashamed at her accusations, Angelique replied, "I am sorry, Dora. I did not mean to pry."

"No. Don't. We have other things to worry about. Will you please hand me that bucket so I can scrub the floors in the kitchen?"

In late 1812, when the season had changed and hurricanes were no longer a threat to a West Indies cruise, the *Julia* set sail with eighty-five men under cover of darkness. *Heart of Allegiance*, though only lightly armed, sailed in convoy. William knew they were headed for some of the most dangerous waters he could have chosen as British ships-of-war crowded the region to protect English trade with Jamaica and South America. It was also the most promising for prizes. The two ships exited the Chesapeake without incident and turned their prows southward.

It was at dawn on the ninth morning at sea, while beating to windward, that the armed clipper came upon its first encounter with what every man aboard hoped was a rich prize.

A sail was discovered upwind, directly in front of them, bearing down with a full press of canvas. To the dismay of *Julia*'s crew, the lookout reported the target to be a British frigate. At her present course and speed she would be in cannon range within minutes. Mounting fifty guns to *Julia*'s thirty-four, and with better-trained guncrews besides, the English vessel could easily outfight the clipper.

Bellowing "All hands to make sail!" Captain Drake let the privateer fall off to run before the wind, and the *Julia* began to flee. While she was gathering momentum, the British ship closed the gap, and ranging shots from English bowchasers caused jets of water to erupt not far astern. A second salvo tore through the mizzen topsail, snapping lines. Within a minute the ruptured sail had torn itself to rags.

William, standing at the stern rail and watching the pursuers, held his breath to see if the loss of one sail would be ruinous. The frigate was gaining, but the wind veered and that change, together with the missing sail, made the *Julia* yaw from her. It was well she did so, for two more cannonballs plunged into the sea where she would have been if still on course. Overhead William saw the topmen scrambling to gather the fragments of ruined canvas and get a replacement rigged, which they did with a speed that only the looming threat of capture or death could induce.

The frigate was forced to fall into the clipper's wake and take up a stern chase. Drake asked William, "Shall we let them have a few of our own?"

"No," was the considered reply. "Not yet."

After thirty anxious minutes and ten more shots that fell astern, it became apparent to William and his crew that they were winning the race. Incredibly *Julia* gained twelve ship lengths in one turn of the glass, and in four hours' time the British warship's hull dropped from sight. In eight hours even its topsails had been swallowed up by the curve of the earth, and the danger was over.

Though it had been an ignoble flight, it was yet regarded as a good omen, and *Julia*'s crew was in high spirits. William, however, began to second-guess his ambitious undertaking, wondering if he had been too rash to carry his private war in what the British Navy regarded as its own pond.

The cold wind blowing in off the Atlantic and into the front doors of Cathedral Hill drove more and more children into Dora's orphanage. Grandfather Sutton's generous financial assistance, so ample-seeming when first tapped, was almost gone, like the remaining leaves on Baltimore's trees. Dora was in the dark-paneled study tucked away off the corner of the converted parsonage's kitchen, hunched over scraps of paper and receipts.

The scratching and scraping of her pen dulled Dora's hearing of the other sounds in the house. As she pored over the diminishing balance, babies cried and cooed and gurgled in the background and a door whooshed open. The wind howled into every nook of the building before the portal was hastily slammed shut, but Dora heard none of it.

The money. She had to find just a few more pennies.

A voice called her from her reverie.

"Dora. Dora! Where are you, *cherie*?" Angelique entered the tiny office space and took in the heap of papers and Dora's ink-spattered sleeves and tear-spattered face. "What is it?" she asked with alarm.

"William always handled the finances, but of course he did not offer to help with this, and I supposed I could do as well . . . and I couldn't exactly beg him to help, could I? And now I'm . . ." Dora recognized she was babbling and caught herself up short. "Developing my own method."

With a throaty chuckle Angelique observed, "A method . . . or a mess, I know not which is the right English, no? But I brought your supper, and Billy wishes to know, will you be home soon?"

"Oh, dear," Dora exclaimed, "is it so late already? I've forgotten the time, and there's Billy's supper to see to, and I'm still so hopelessly muddled that I can't think how I'll get home soon. I . . ."

"Calm yourself," Angelique said soothingly. "Billy, he is at my house and fed to the ears already. Take a minute to nourish yourself too."

As if the thought of supper could not even be entertained, Dora said, "It's the finances, really . . . not just the bookkeeping, I mean. We're almost out of Grandfather's assistance, and I must replenish it somehow or all this . . ." She swept her arm around the orphanage in a gesture of helplessness. "The war has driven up prices, and we have more children to care for than I imagined. With such harsh weather, what will become of the babies?"

"*Oui,* Dora. With you always it is the babies."

There was an inflection in Angelique's words that Dora did not like. She tilted her head with dismay. "Angelique?"

"Albert, he is in Washington, and I worry for him constantly. But are you not the least concerned for William? Do you banish him from your thoughts as you have from your heart? He is at war, Dora! At war and at sea. *Mon Dieu!* Can you not spare some regard, or how can you sleep at night? My heart . . . my whole self . . . longs for my dear Albert."

Dora sighed raggedly. "Angelique, I don't know what to say. I miss William. I *have* missed him. I need comforting; needed it when he was still here, and when he could not or would not care, I looked to be needed elsewhere . . . here, with the children. How can you be so cruel as to punish me with such words? Not today! Not today!"

In an instant Angelique and Dora, sniffling, plunged into each other's embrace; each asking the other for forgiveness and pledging their friendship anew.

"I pray for William every night," Dora said. "I wish I had him to advise me, but I have been afraid to admit it for fear of breaking!" Dora wiped her tears, smearing ink across her cheek. Angelique laughed, blotting the smudge with her thumb to show her sister-in-law what she had done.

Then a sturdy resolve came into Dora's eyes, and she straightened. "I am better," she said. "I was sitting here feeling sorry for myself and not wanting to have to struggle but now I know what must be done, and without delay."

"What, *cherie*?"

"I am going to Boston, to the Abolitionist Society headquartered there. Surely they will listen. Surely they will want to help the orphans of slaves."

By Dora's reckoning, she had approximately one month left to acquire the funding necessary to prevent the orphanage from being bankrupted. She approached Grandfather Sutton about going to Boston to speak to a group called the Quaker Abolitionists.

"Grandfather Sutton, you have been entirely

generous. The children are well cared for, and today we placed thirty babies. The building is at capacity. We knew your funds could not last forever, and I have been thinking . . ." Dora drew a breath.

Grandfather Sutton interrupted. "My dear Dora, *you* are the one who has been generous. You saw the needs of the helpless ones and met them and more. True, your allotted funds are dwindling. What do you propose?"

The kindness and reassurance ever-present in Grandfather Sutton's eyes and presence bolstered her courage.

"I have been thinking that perhaps I should go north to Boston to speak with the abolitionists." Dora's words tumbled out in a rush. "I thought that of any people those would be the ones to see the importance of this orphanage."

Grandfather knit his brows tightly. "Dora, you know what implications going to them would have. While we have been frowned upon in this town for starting this home for orphans, going north, to a group outspoken in their opposition to the South's 'peculiar institution' would be the ultimate red flag before the bull. In place of criticism you may find yourself facing open opposition."

Dora leaned forward, determination steeling her frame. "Grandfather, the people of Baltimore have turned their backs for years upon these babies. Even when our doors opened, they have not offered any support. You alone have acted with a Christian heart by providing the financial means." Righteousness stole into her voice, edging her words with precision. "We have worked diligently in God's service to feed and clothe the babies this society has chosen to forget. He remembers them all, and I will not turn away."

Grandfather straightened with a smile. "Bravo, my dear! If you can speak with such conviction to me, you are certainly prepared to face what is to come. I have contacts in Boston who will assist you in connecting with the right people."

Leading Dora to a mahogany armchair, Grandfather Sutton began listing names of those with whom she should speak. In addition, he would write a letter of introduction that would ensure she be seen. With such backing, Grandfather Sutton offered Dora what she was seeking most: his faith in her ability to continue to provide for the children.

Skirting the edges of the shipping lanes carried the *Julia* and *Allegiance* past all kinds of targets, but in every case the British merchantmen were accompanied by warships. What William needed was a lone vessel, cut off from the protection of frigates.

It was nearing nightfall when sails were sighted from the masthead. Moments later the rails of the clipper were lined with men peering into the gathering gloom, eagerly watching to see if the newcomer was alone.

It was.

Julia was upwind. It was therefore her choice to bring on a battle. Captain Drake muttered, "Be our luck if she's American! Do we fire a warning shot?"

"No," was William's response, eyeing the quarry through his glass. "She's a hermaphrodite rig. See? Both square sails and a fore-and-aft rig. If we can take her without wrecking her, so much the better. Since we're upwind and up sun both, they'll be squinting to make us out. Let's see how our disguise holds. Signal her to heave-to for news."

In response to the signal from *Julia* colors broke out at the brig's masthead. Drake said with disgust, "French flag. Not a lawful prize."

William retorted, "English built, or I don't know Dover shipyards! And just look at that over-long bowsprit. You could never disguise that one. Lay us to windward about pistol-shot away. Prepare the starboard battery, but don't run out till I give the word."

When the maneuver was completed, the two vessels lay rocking in the swell no more than fifty yards apart. "What ship is that?" William called through a speaking trumpet.

"*Equalitie,*" was the reply. "Marseilles! *Parlez vous Francais?*"

"Right! And we're a Mississippi keelboat," William said to Drake. Raising the speaking trumpet again he shouted, "Stand by to be boarded."

"*Non!* It is not permitted!" A score of marksmen lined the side of the other vessel, armed with muskets. Another twelve took station in the rigging. Fore and aft a pair of swivel cannons were pivoted to point toward the *Julia.* "Who do you think you are?" The adopted French accent had somehow disappeared.

"I think," William yelled back, "that we are the American privateer *Julia,* and you are my prisoner! Run out the guns!" The starboard gunports dropped open with a crash, and a row of cannon muzzles gleamed dully in the setting sun.

Instead of facing merely a clipper ship, the crew of the other vessel found themselves contemplating enough lethal force to tear their ship to pieces; and there was nothing they could do about it.

William watched as a hasty conference took place on the other deck. Apparently the captain wanted to fight, but his officers persuaded him otherwise.

"Brig *Wessex*. One month out of Portsmouth loaded with gunpowder, shot, and cannons!" William sat reading the captured ship's manifest aloud to Captain Drake. Both men looked at each other with relief.

"No wonder she surrendered," Drake observed. "Our broadside wasn't needed. One lucky salvo would have blown them to kingdom come."

"At pistol-shot? We would have accompanied them to see Saint Peter," William replied.

"What now?"

"I want you to have charge of the *Wessex*," William said. "Take twenty-five men to guard the prisoners. I'll assume command here and continue the cruise."

"I'm to sail her back to Baltimore?"

"No. The British blockade will be tightening, and she's too rich a prize to risk losing back to them. Take her to Lisbon. I'll send *Allegiance* too. Gerald Fussel will see that she's properly disposed of."

The rumbling January coach ride from Baltimore to Boston lasted three days; three days in which Dora planned how to approach the people who might provide the only support the orphanage would receive.

Yet standing in the foyer of one Mrs. Charlotte Hollingsworth, her confidence wavered. So much was riding on this first meeting, and Dora feared she might fail. The childless widow Hollingsworth was the sole heir to her husband's vast commercial fortune made in banking and providing insurance for seagoing ventures. She was rumored to be as wealthy as the Lees of Virginia, and known to be an outspoken abolitionist.

A maid returned and ushered Dora into the sunny sitting room, where every corner was laced with fragrant bouquets of dried flowers: violet and lavender. The chill of the winter outdoors vanished with their light scent.

Mrs. Hollingsworth sat reading a paper intently as Dora entered. With barely a glance for her visitor, Mrs. Hollingsworth waved at a chair to indicate where Dora should sit. Dora perched on the edge.

"Missus Sutton, is it? I hear you have a request to make of me," began Mrs. Hollingsworth.

Dora smiled, relieved Mrs. Hollingsworth would allow her to be direct, and handed her Grandfather Sutton's letter.

"Your reputation of support for abolition is known even in Baltimore, Mrs. Hollingsworth. We have begun an orphanage for the babies born into slavery who would be left to die as their mothers are sold away. I have come seeking financial backing from the Boston abolitionists to help provide for these children."

"Why should we support a slave nursery?" said Mrs. Hollingsworth, sniffing. "Won't these children simply be slaves when they reach maturity?"

Shocked, Dora replied, "No, indeed. You have my assurance that the basis of the orphanage is to provide the residents with freedom. They are babies left on our doorstep or purchased from slavers with our funds. Part of our expenses lies in the paperwork to ensure their freed status," explained Dora. "We have obtained a court order specifying that foundlings raised by our home become the property of the home, but it is our intent that every one of them will be freed."

Mrs. Hollingsworth adjusted her spectacles. "Missus Sutton, our group is determined to contribute to the ending of human bondage in this country. We came together to provide a resounding voice exposing the evils of slavery in our society. Our support would be contingent upon maintaining this ideal. Are you prepared to face what your Baltimore society will say regarding your involvement with us?" she finished with a raised eyebrow.

"Missus Hollingsworth, 'my' society, as you call it, has had ample opportunity to provide for these, God's children, and has chosen not to. I refuse to allow them to perish or to be raised in slavery. Your group can financially save this orphanage or look away for political reasons, as much of the world has. I merely sought the chance to speak with you and ask your aid." Dora paused to allow her words weight.

Mrs. Hollingsworth's grim lips softened into a

smile, and she extended a gloved hand. "Missus Sutton, you already had my somewhat skeptical admiration. Now you have my endorsement. Our group will be meeting next week, and you may speak. But I insist you spend the remainder of your stay as my guest. I wish to learn more of this enlightened young woman and the ways I can assist her in her orphanage."

A bubbling laugh escaped Dora as relief rushed to the surface. Her children would be saved. God's babies would survive.

CHAPTER 10

A lbert Sutton crashed through the door of Secretary Monroe's Washington office without
knocking or waiting to be invited. The February
news Albert received from Canada had lit him up
like a fuse to a keg of gunpowder. "What is this
they did? *Sacre bleu!* Have they no sense? Are they
savages, like red Indians?" Albert said, barely able
to control his outrage.

"Calm yourself, Albert," Secretary Monroe
instructed. "It was a military operation that got out
of hand."

Albert gritted his teeth. "Those hooligans decided
to loot York and then burn it to the ground?"

"General Dearborn reported that he could not
control his men after they found a scalp hanging in
the headquarters of the British government. It was
a child's scalp!"

"*Diable!*" Albert replied, turning pale and sitting down abruptly. "And I thought I had seen the atrocities of war in Austria."

Secretary Monroe regarded his protégé with sympathetic understanding. "We have," he said after a period of silence, "at last managed to reverse our misfortunes in the land war. At the same time we continue to do well at sea."

In December 1812 the *Constitution*, widely referred to by its nickname, *Old Ironsides*, had battered the British frigate *Java* into submission. In every corner of the globe, from the South Pacific to the Irish Sea, American commerce raiders successfully preyed on British shipping. William and the *Julia* accounted for a dozen prizes. This hampering of British trade did little to directly impact the American war, but certainly distressed English businessmen.

"Those firebrands in the British Parliament," Secretary Monroe continued, "who thought they would teach this upstart nation a quick lesson, must be spinning. Our spies in England tell us there is a substantial and growing public outcry for a negotiated peace."

Albert indicated his agreement, then wondered aloud if the wanton American destruction of the capital of Upper Canada would not backfire and stiffen British resolve to continue the war.

Monroe added nothing to that thought. It was clear he had already reached that despairing conclusion, but regarded it as too late to remedy.

As Albert watched Monroe's face, he saw the secretary evidently struggle with a decision and then reach a conclusion. "There is one other point of news not yet widely known," Monroe said. "Napoleon has been badly beaten in Russia. His troops are in retreat, decimated and demoralized, while the British close in on France from Spain. It is thought that the European war will be ended in a year or less." He left the conclusion hanging in the air for Albert to finish.

"Freeing thousands of British troops to come here," Albert summarized.

"After what has happened in Russia and at York, we must expect British attacks in force on Baltimore and here at Washington. We," Monroe repeated, underscoring the plural with emphasis, "must expect such attacks, even if no one else does."

By late winter 1813, William and the *Julia* were tired, worn, and in need of harbor and rest. Though intact in vital respects, the privateer had sustained cumulative damage because of her numerous encounters. In her half-year career she had successfully captured twenty English ships but lost eight more. She had experienced enough brushes with Royal Navy vessels that she was leaking almost as fast as the pumps could empty her hold. So many of her spars had been jury-rigged that a single cannonball striking the wrong stay might send all her masts overboard in a body.

Julia was cruising off the Azores, a group of Portuguese-owned islands in the Atlantic that were a thousand miles from anywhere. Captain Drake, returned from convoying more prizes to neutral Portugal, suggested it was time to put in for resupply, perhaps even return to Baltimore.

"Not yet," William returned. "We have enough fight left in us for one more engagement before we cry 'Hold.'"

Drake, unconvinced but obedient, deferred to the owner's wishes.

So it was ten days later, when a lone sail was sighted at one bell of the first dogwatch, William ordered a pursuit and another chase began. The late-afternoon wind was steady from the southeast and the course of the unknown vessel due north. It was clear from her lack of evasive maneuvers that *Julia*'s presence was as yet undetected. "There's no moon tonight," Drake pointed out. "We cannot catch her before dark unless we clap on sail. But if we're spotted, she'll keep out of reach till after sunset and then double back. What do you want to do?"

William noted the angle of the sun and the board of the knot log that recorded *Julia*'s speed as a constant six knots. "She'll reduce sail at sunset," he suggested. "Every proper, cautious merchant captain does. Let's drop back far enough to keep her in sight. At sundown we'll match her course and speed and see if we can't close with her after dawn when she can't give us the slip. Call me if anything changes," he added. "It may be a long night's watch. I'm going below to grab some sleep while I can."

It was with considerable surprise that William was awakened after sunset with the news that not only was the quarry holding to her course; she was showing a light.

"A light?" he questioned. "Doesn't her captain know there's a war on?"

Once again Drake and William compared notes. "It could be a trap," Captain Drake suggested. "We never got a good look at her. What if she's a warship or decoying us into an ambush?"

"Can she have gotten any better look at us?" William returned. "How would they know what they've caught? No, I say we keep following."

Below, in Drake's cabin, careful *not* to show a betraying sign of light, William pored over the charts. Their present location was between thirty-nine and forty degrees of north latitude and just over thirty-one degrees of west longitude. The sole landfall for which the quarry could be making appeared to be the island of Santa Cruz de Flores, but just after midnight Santa Cruz fell astern. That left only the tiny, seven-square-mile rock known as Corvo.

"That's it," William decided. The lookout had reported in an unnecessarily cautious whisper that the other ship was slowing and altering course east. "She's putting in to Corvo."

"Curse the luck!" Drake exclaimed. "We've been wasting our time following a neutral Portuguese ship. Probably damaged and working to repair."

"I don't think so," William argued. "If she's Portuguese and in need of repairs, why bypass Santa Cruz? Set a course for the opposite side of the island," he decided. "I'll take a shoreparty overland and see what this is about."

William, his face smeared with burnt cork, carried a pair of pistols thrust through his belt. He commanded one of *Julia*'s longboats and Drake commanded the other. Though they landed on the opposite side of Corvo from the position chosen by the mystery ship, the oars had been muffled, and no one spoke except in a hoarse muttering.

Assembling his men, William warned them against any noise or firing until they were sure of their target. "Remember," he said, "this is merely a scouting expedition until I say differently."

Drake shared one final thought. "What if it's another American privateer put in for repairs?"

His grin showing as a lighter patch in the darkness, William replied, "Then we'll ask if they can spare some coffee."

Crossing the narrow islet took only a few minutes and a campfire revealed the presence of men from the other vessel. A hasty reconnoiter convinced William there was no guard, and no treachery was to be expected. "Let's get closer," he proposed. Soon a ring of twenty men had closed around the fire, while William himself crawled to within ten paces.

The sailors from the other ship made no pretense

at being silent. "Blimey!" one of them spouted. "Ain't it enough that we gotta pump all bloody day long to keep the *Duchess* afloat without we gotta work all night too?"

"Ah, shut ye gob," returned another. "You ain't workin', Chester, I am. But it's high time you did. Get back to work stitchin' on them bellows."

"All right, Darby, don't get sore."

Minutes later William had heard enough. "They're English!" he told Drake after scooting backward to rejoin his men. "That ship is the English privateer *Duchess of Newcastle*, the same one that's been giving our whaling ships such a hard time. She's lately back from the South Atlantic and damaged her rudder mechanism in a blow. She secretly put in here to repair it so as not to give away her presence in these waters."

Every American present knew what an unexpected opportunity this was. If they could destroy, or better yet, capture, an opposing privateer, they would not only enrich themselves, but strike a direct blow in the war.

"Right," Drake said, offering the single word that summarized the whole crew's commitment. "What's the drill?"

Within an hour, as William had been certain

would be true, one of the fireside workers left off blacksmithing and retreated into the dunes to answer a call of nature. A minute later, the English sailor was knocked unconscious, and William was wearing his jacket and cap.

"What's the matter, Tim?" Darby inquired. "Get lost, did yer?"

William did not reply until standing in front of the remaining five Englishmen, whereupon he whipped out the pistols and leveled them. "Stand easy, men," he ordered. "Make no sounds, and no one gets hurt! But let one of you so much as peep, and I'll blow his head off."

Within minutes Darby, Chester, and the rest were bound and gagged back of the dunes, the operation carried out so carefully that a watcher from the *Duchess* would not notice anything amiss.

"I'll take their launch," William told Drake, "and eight of our men. I'll give you one hour. You and the others run like madmen back to our boats and row like crazy around to the far side of the *Duchess*. When you hear the fight break out, come boiling over the rail."

When an hour had passed, William and his picked men shoved the launch into the surf and rowed for the *Duchess*. All the while William wondered if he had given Drake enough time to get in position. It would be a lonely feeling indeed to try and capture an enemy of perhaps one hundred men with just nine!

"Ahoy, Chester," called a voice from the deck of the English raider when the launch's return was detected. "What're you doin' back?"

In his best East London rasp, William replied, "Blinkin' idiot forgot me second bloody tool pouch. Can't do naught without it."

"But why din't ya send some 'un?" the lookout inquired. "Captain'll have yer back for shoe leather."

"Look sharp," someone else called. "There's too many men in that boat!"

By then *Julia*'s men were swarming aboard, pistols and cutlasses waving. "Julia!" William called by way of an identifying battle cry. "To me!"

Shouts, pistol shots, and the ring of steel on steel answered his cry.

As he swung himself over the railing, a figure in the dark swung a cutlass at his face. Catching the blow on his pistol barrel, William parried the thrust, then discharged the weapon at his attacker. His opponent screamed and dropped his weapon.

Beside him one of his sailors was beset by two enemies at once. William shot one man in the arm.

Next he threw the empty pistol against the other's forehead, then retrieved an abandoned sword and forced the man to vault into the ocean to escape being skewered.

From the opposite side of the ship, both forward and aft, came the responding shouts of "Julia! Julia!" Drake and the others were on time.

The night erupted with the explosion of a rail-mounted swivel cannon and dissolved into the shrieks of a score of men wounded by its shot. But who fired? Whose were the screams?

The answer was obtained shortly when an English voice commanded, "*Duchess*'s men! This is Captain Alban. Throw down your weapons!"

The captured English skipper and his men were soon herded belowdecks and imprisoned. Drake then returned to William's side. "Now we have to put in to port," he said. "Sailing the prize and guarding this lot will leave you too shorthanded for operating *Julia*."

Smiling, William said, "Lisbon. If we're questioned, we'll say that *Duchess* captured *us*!"

It had been seven years since William was aboard the *H.M.S. Victory,* headed for the Battle of

Trafalgar, the memory of which had never ceased to give him chills. But now, as he steered past the Straits of Gibraltar, he felt afraid for another reason. When the British beat the French on that day off the coast of Spain, they gained control over the waters of Europe, from the North Sea to the corners of the Mediterranean. This was wonderful while William considered himself to be English, and remained tolerable after he had renounced George as his king. But the year was no longer 1805 or 1806, nor was it the blissfully ignorant summer of 1812. Now late in the spring of 1813, war, red war, continued over half the globe. The threat was no longer the French, but his former colleagues, the redcoats of the Royal Marines.

Why had he not thought of it sooner, he wondered. Avoiding Baltimore and the blockade of the American coast *seemed* prudent, but sailing toward the coast of the Iberian peninsula could be the hottest of all cauldrons to cruise into since the British would keep a strong watch over Napoleon's forces there.

The honest part of William's mind inquired if he had made this decision out of prudence or had his caution been blinded by the thoughts of Michelle Braganza. *What am I thinking?* He cursed himself, not even noticing the beauty of the sea, which had once so enchanted him. Now he seemed lost in the beauty of a particular woman. But all the time a drumroll of warning, like the call to battle aboard a ship-of-the-line, signaled his internal conflict. *I have a wife and child at home. Who am I kidding? . . . Myself,* he concluded.

The plaque stating the name of his ship was removed and once more replaced with *Feliciatas Julia.* The captured vessel had been re-rigged to change her appearance. American colors were run down, and flags of Portugal flew in their places. As long as he was not stopped and searched, as long as the prize was not recognized, as long as the English prisoners were not heard . . . The list went on and on, though there was no changing his mind, no heading back.

Contrary to his fears, the passage to Portugal and Lisbon was made safely. The ships arrived at night, which helped to conceal their identities. Once in port William speedily found transportation to the Braganza estate.

From the top of the hill William witnessed two of the largest English frigates sail slowly past on the horizon. He wondered if they might stop, but the cab did not wait for him to find out. Past the mansions and ruins they traveled, finally arriving at the gatehouse.

First inquiring as to his identity in Portuguese, the gateman asked again in English, "Who are you?"

"I am William Sutton of the American Coastal Shipping Company. I am a friend and business associate of Carlos Braganza, and it is urgent I see him right away."

Holding a lamp into the carriage, the man scowled at William. "He will not be happy if I wake him up."

"It is of no consequence. He will see me. Open these gates at once!"

The man must have believed William's insistence, for he opened the gates and sent word for Senhor Braganza to be roused.

Minutes later, Carlos appeared in his nightdress.

"William!" Braganza cried. "What is it? I had no word."

"I'm sorry, Carlos," William said apologetically. "Privateering has led to more clandestine arrivals and departures."

"Yes! And you have made brilliant and wealthy conquests, yes?"

William acknowledged that the exploits had

been productive and mentioned the latest-captured prize ship he was delivering. "I have seized a highly valuable ship. I wish for you to act as agent."

Carlos patted him on the shoulder. "I shall do this, but you should not have come yourself. You put yourself in danger to come here. There are Royal Navy ships everywhere."

"I know this, sir . . ."

"Forgive me. Please come in." Carlos led him into the study, where the two sat down. A servant appeared with a lamp and left. "Can I offer you food or drink?"

"No, thank you. I realize I am in jeopardy, but . . ." Suddenly William flushed. How could he speak what had truly attracted him there?

Carlos Braganza saved William the bother of explaining. His teeth shimmered in the dim light. "Ah, William!" he teased slyly. "You are in love with my Michelle, I think. The dashing knight of the sea steals in at midnight for a rendezvous with his lady, yes? But alas! She is not here."

William found himself on the edge of his seat. "She's not?"

"No, I regret to inform you that she is in Brazil, at our plantation there. These months in the northern hemisphere have been too cold for my hotblooded little girl."

William's entire purpose sank. He had come all the way, risking his own life and the lives of his crew, his ship. The urge to leave overwhelmed him, and he rose to his feet. "I must go."

"So soon?" Braganza was taken by surprise.

"Yes, the risk may be too severe for my ship and my crew if I wait past dawn."

Carlos appeared to understand. He patted William on the back. "It is no problem. Gerald Fussel and I will take care of your prize, and when I see you in Brazil soon, we will settle up."

"The English crew remains aboard, locked in the hold."

"That is no problem for me. I will take them to the prisoner exchange. What can I say? I am a middleman. They will not balk at their freedom."

William smiled, tired-eyed, though inside he wondered how he could keep others from finding out why he had really come.

Anticipating William's remaining concern, Braganza asked, "And how are your provisions aboard . . the *Julia,* I presume?"

"The *Feliciatas Julia.*"

Carlos grinned with remembrance. "Ah, yes! How very like my own son you could be!"

"We are running short on food and water."

"It is no problem. I will have your ship loaded with fresh stores within the hour. Four more and you will be under way again." Carlos scribbled on two sheets of fine stationery.

"That will be wonderful. Thank you," William said with sincere gratitude.

"We are partners, eh? And it will get better. If we had time we would drink a toast to a long-lasting war with many profits. But see here: let us meet again in Rio. I've written details of the date when I will be there myself . . . and a tiny favor by way of a cargo I wish you to transport for me."

Drink a toast to a long war? William wondered. "Thank you again, Carlos. You have been a friend to me, above and beyond the call of business."

Braganza handed the folded order for provisions to him at the door. "I shall see you in a few months, William, and will give your love to my daughter . . . until you can do so yourself."

Back in the carriage rumbling toward the harbor, William could not shake the load of worry and guilt from the visit.

Recalling the papers Carlos had given him, William opened them. One was an order to the Braganza provisioner to load the *Julia*. The second was an invitation to use Braganza harbor facilities at the port of Rio when *Julia* needed them.

Rio? he pondered, attracted to the idea.

Braganza's provisioners took over at dockside, and as the man had said, within hours, the clipper was restocked and cast off. The remains of the night may have protected William from immediately being plunged back into the war, but did nothing to relieve the warring inside.

CHAPTER 11

Dora's newfound self-confidence allowed her to assert herself in bargaining, but still she did not enjoy it. Feeling that the stall holders were out to cheat her, she girded herself as if for battle every time she ventured forth to shop.

Angelique, on the other hand, continued to relish the challenge. Wielding her feminine wit like a sword, Angelique approached merchants up and down the halls of Lexington Market, alternately coy and scolding. A conspiratorial wink, a warm smile, Angelique always left the sellers happy at the encounter, even if she did get the necessary provender for the orphanage at less than half the asking prices.

"Good day, Monsieur Max," she greeted the

elderly, wizened livestock dealer. "Business is well with you, yes?"

"Business ain't what I wished it was, ma'am," Max admitted. "But it's a pleasure to see the way you light up this place. What can I do for you today?"

"Nothing, I do not think," Angelique demurred. "I merely stopped because I see that goat, the one with the large tan patch on her shoulder. She is the same beast from two weeks, yes? No one buys goats anymore?"

"Feed bein' so hard to ship, what with the blockade," Max said. "I got a lot in her. Can't afford to let her go cheap. Good milker too."

"So?" Angelique queried with a disbelieving note. "She does not look . . . how is it . . . deep in the bag? She is not good for more than two quarts a day, I think."

Puffing out his cheeks, Max said in an offended tone, "Four, ma'am, four! Milk enough to feed kids, make cheese with, raise hogs on what's left."

Squinting and opening her handbag as if counting change, Angelique inquired, "And what would be your asking price, Max?"

"For you, ma'am," the dealer said gallantly,

"two and a half dollars. Cain't go lower without takin' food outta my own babies' mouths."

"But no? Monsieur Max, your babies will always be welcome to get a meal from us. They need never go hungry, eh?"

With that Angelique hoisted her skirts with one hand and grabbed the top rail of the pen with the other. She did not see the pair of toughs lounging against a support pole watching her. She perched momentarily, scanned the straw for a safe place to land, then dropped into the pen. Circling the animal in question, she studied it.

"Is anything wrong, ma'am?"

Flipping her hand with indecision, Angelique finally replied, "This one, she is long of hoof and horn. Maybe no more than one season left, yes? And the other there, with the two kids, she is a new mother and not proven?"

Max acknowledged the truth of the assertions.

"The problem, you see," Angelique continued, "is that the orphanage needs *two* goats. We have enough older children now that it is time for more goat's milk. But the most we can afford is two dollars for both."

Before Max could protest that this was highway robbery, the two rough-looking men flanked him and confronted Angelique over the fence rail. "You're from that nigger orphanage, ain't ya?" the taller of the two demanded.

Ignoring the coarse talk and the speakers, Angelique carried on as if nothing else had transpired. "Two dollars, Max?"

"Not too good to keep black rats alive, but too good to speak to us, eh Saul?"

"Right, Quince."

"You two leave Missus Sutton alone," Max responded.

"Shut up, you," Saul ordered. "You stink like a goat. This town is tight as a drum . . . no work, no charity . . . while this so-called lady is takin' money to feed nigger babies. What say we show her what we think of that, Quince?"

Angelique backed to the far corner of the pen, but the second ruffian circled around to keep her from escaping that way.

"You two better . . . ," Max began.

"And I said, you stink!" Saul repeated, knocking Max down and then throwing the goat seller into a water trough.

"Leave him alone!" Angelique shouted.

"Gonna make me?" said Saul, sneering. "No? Well, I'm comin' in after you, then."

Saul got one foot up on the bottom rail and the other boot across the top rail when a hand dropped on his shoulder. "I didn't hear you ask permission."

"Huh? Who's gonna . . ." Saul's question never got completed, nor did his head get more than halfway round to view the newcomer, because at that moment Albert's fist landed on Saul's cheekbone. The force of the blow propelled the hooligan over the fence. By chance his forehead smacked into the single square of stone pavement that was not covered with straw, knocking him cold.

Without even attempting to help his friend, Quince ran.

Seizing an ax handle that Max used to prod his livestock, Albert whirled it end over end. The butt of the hickory stick struck Quince in the back, causing him to collide face-first with a pillar.

Albert assisted Angelique in recrossing the railing. "I am always returning to rescue you, it seems," he said. Then to Max, who stood dripping but unharmed, he said, "Do you need help dealing with those two?"

"Not a bit of it!" Max replied, retrieving the ax handle and thumping it into his palm. "But ma'am," he said, remembering, "what about them two goats? Two dollars, you said?"

Batting her lashes, Angelique responded, "Why thank you, Monsieur Max. You will please deliver them to the orphanage tomorrow and . . . throw in three sacks of feed, won't you?"

In answer to the delighted inquiries from his wife, children, and Grandfather Sutton, Albert acknowledged that yes, he was home unexpectedly from Washington, but that even better, he was home to stay. Dora, Billy, and little Allie, also present at the family gathering, likewise welcomed him warmly.

Dora asked if there was any news of William and the *Julia*.

"Not for several months," Albert acknowledged apologetically. "It is widely said that she was responsible for the capture of a notorious English raiding vessel. But since then, nothing but rumors! *Julia* has been reported everywhere from Halifax to New South Wales, but when I try to run down the truth, *poof!* It vanishes like smoke."

"Oh," Dora said sadly. "I just thought . . ."

"But do not worry!" Angelique urged. "Surely no news is good news, eh?"

The women removed the children to the parlor,

allowing Grandfather Sutton and Albert to talk privately.

"Now I can tell you why I am home," Albert said, "but I would rather it remained between us."

"Of course, my boy," Grandfather Sutton asserted.

"I am still working for Secretary Monroe. He and I believe that by next spring or summer at the latest, the British will have enough troops shipped here from Europe to launch a major army campaign."

"And where will this attack take place?" When Albert did not reply, Grandfather Sutton concluded for him, "Here on the Chesapeake, of course. That will keep us guessing while allowing them to attack Washington, Annapolis, or Baltimore."

"And I am here to organize the defense of Baltimore," Albert said. "Against Fort McHenry a direct assault is unlikely, but a flanking movement could come from either east or west." Albert paused and then asked, "Do you know a man named Fulton? Robert Fulton?"

"Know *of* him," Grandfather Sutton replied. "Met him once in London in the late eighties. Bit of an inventor. Engineer chap. Works with steam power, I think."

"Just so," Albert replied. "He was in Washington

last week, lobbying for funds for a secret invention. Some sort of steam-propelled gunship."

"Steam warship?" Grandfather repeated, incredulous. "Fire and gunpowder together? Preposterous! Too dangerous by far. Never work. Why do you ask about him?"

"He is coming here next week to meet with me, at Secretary Monroe's insistence," Albert noted. "Another secret weapon, I think, but that is all I know so far."

"Be wary of him," Grandfather warned. "After more money, no doubt. Did he get funding?"

"Eh?"

"Money. You said he was seeking government funds."

"Oh," Albert said. "Yes. Forty thousand dollars."

Grandfather Sutton whistled his amazement and wrinkled his nose with displeasure at the profligate spendthrifts in Washington, but Albert had already shifted topics. "You know Angelique was accosted in the market today," he said.

"Yes," Grandfather Sutton acknowledged. "No harm done though?"

Albert reflected on the memory of the two sprawled hooligans. "Not to Angelique," he said.

"But what caused it? Angelique says they made comments about the orphanage?"

Passing his veined hand through his thinning hair, Grandfather Sutton replied, "It's this blasted blockade. Trade has lowered to a crawl. Business is off, prices are up, people are out of work. You know how it is: in hard times people always hunt for someone to blame. In this case, instead of blaming the Royal Navy, they blame free black laborers who will work cheaper than white men. By extension, you see, men of low intelligence and still less skill see a larger crop of free Negroes as a threat."

"Is there danger to the orphanage?"

Grandfather studied the portraits of his dead son and daughter-in-law, Albert's father and mother, which hung over the mantel. "Real enough that I'm glad you are home, my boy," he said.

The man Hooey ushered into Grandfather Sutton's parlor had a high forehead, a shock of thick brown hair, wide-set eyes, and a double chin. Robert Fulton's mannerisms, like his speech, were economical and pointed.

"Hear you have charge of Baltimore defenses,"

he asserted to Albert after introductions were complete.

"Of their construction," Albert said. "Not their command."

"What are you going to do about the British warships?"

"Do about them? They cannot sail into the guns of Fort McHenry," Albert suggested.

"No," Fulton agreed, "but they can lay off and pound the fort with their long guns. Can't give them that freedom."

"So what *can* be done about them?" Albert asked. "I have neither the time nor the funds to build batteries lower down the channel."

"Ah,' Fulton said, hunching forward. "Have you heard of Burnell's Turtle?"

Certain he was dealing with someone more than a trifle odd, Albert slowly breathed out and said, "No."

"Submarine boat. More like a barrel. Man inside turns a crank, which turns a propeller, goes undetected up to a British ship and attaches a bomb, then goes away before . . ." Here Fulton slapped his hands together with such force that Albert, who was likewise leaning forward, was startled and jumped back.

The inventor seemed not to notice anything amiss and continued, "I've refined it. Better propeller. Copper-plated. Ballast valve for descent. Air pump for ascent. It'll work too. Going to try it in New London. Here too?"

It took Albert a moment to realize this last volley of clipped words was a question. He finally responded, "Not me, sir. I know nothing of submersible boats."

"Ah, well." Fulton sighed. "Currents too much here anyway. But you can use some of my patented torpedoes. Screw into hulls and . . ."

This time Albert was prepared and leaned back in time to escape the force of Fulton's gunshot hand clap.

The war continued to be a back-and-forth battle for superiority on land and sea. His temper growing increasingly ragged, British Admiral Cochrane ordered the destruction of some New England towns; others he allowed to escape razing after paying indemnities.

Then in September 1813, a significant American victory occurred: the Battle of Lake Erie, won by Admiral Oliver Hazard Perry, ended any

British threat from that direction for the rest of the war.

Despite William's continued success as a privateer, the British blockade of U.S. ports was expanded. Originally there had been only enough sentry ships to guard the Chesapeake Bay. As time passed, more and more Royal Navy vessels were released from duty in the Baltic and Mediterranean and dispatched to patrol the Atlantic, the Gulf of Mexico, and the Caribbean trade routes. Baltimore, Charleston harbor, Boston, New York, and New London were bottled up.

In retaliation, William and his brother privateer captains imposed a blockade of sorts on England, even issuing a mock proclamation to that effect. They continued to prey on British shipping, from whalers loaded with oil to East Indiamen laden with spice and silk.

But for his success, William at last was running out of places to repair and resupply his ship. Portugal was no longer safe and no American harbor was deemed possible.

"It's time," he announced to Captain Drake. "We're going to Rio."

CHAPTER 12

———— ❦ ————

The late October carriage ride up from Guanabara Bay led into rounded and forested hills that shut out William's view of Rio de Janeiro. The world appeared green and vast and nothing else. The rocking motion of the coach was shiplike enough that William did not have the typically unsettled experience of a sailor ashore; he slept. He did not see the countryside change from hills to mile after mile of sugarcane plantation until he was awakened by the absence of movement.

He had been dreaming of Michelle Braganza, and he awoke with a guilty start to find her smirking indulgently at his sleep-stupefied features. Suffused with an embarrassed flush, William was certain Michelle could read his every thought. She was, as always, dressed in an alluring fashion:

loose-fitting, shimmering silk blouse above tight, leather riding breeches. A flat-crowned hat, set about with silver conchas, was set back on her head, and she laughed into his face at his confusion.

"Welcome, Senhor William!" Grasping William's hands in hers she propelled him from the carriage, kissed him on the lips, and then thrust him away before his brain had stopped spinning. "Go," she ordered. "Manuela will show you to your room for you to bathe and change into dress better suited for this climate and for riding!"

Refreshed and attired as a wealthy horseman, William was brought by the wizened, brown-skinned maid to a terrace at which Michelle and her father were seated. While the two men greeted each other, Michelle poured William a tall glass of red wine mixed with fruit juices, demanding he drink it off at once. When he had obeyed, she refilled the glass again, nor was it ever more than half-empty during the two hours they visited on the patio.

William was treated to a Brazilian lunch of stewed beans, brown rice, and flat bread. Braganza bragged about the productivity of the countryside and how a man with a little money and a lot of ambition could achieve a huge fortune. William nodded politely, all the while being alternately distracted by Michelle's revealing shirt and form-hugging trousers.

Braganza chatted on, promising to show William the secrets to making millions in cash. It was, he said, like coining sunlight into gold. "The sun, the rains, the way the cane shoots up!" he said. "The way the brokers bid against each other for our sugar! There is only one bit of management needed, but this I will show you in person." At a snap of his fingers, a pair of richly furnished horses, obviously saddled and awaiting the signal, were led to Senhor Braganza and his guest. Michelle pretended to pout at being left behind, but when William glanced back from atop the prancing bay, Michelle was staring after him and blew him a kiss.

It was not far to the plantation's sugar mill, where thousands of African slaves did every task in the production of sugar and tobacco from planting to refining. The two men dismounted at the entry to a long, pole-supported roofed structure without walls, near endless green fields of sugarcane.

Braganza, who had not stopped pointing to various aspects of his success since they left the house, continued to expound. "The soil and the rainfall and the sunshine require no effort, no large application of intellect. But sugar is a difficult mistress to satisfy. Her needs require constant attention and labor. The greatest gift of God is the power of a man to control other men. You see, the weak-willed and soft-minded individual must submit to the stronger-willed and sharper mind. It is life's beauty. Two men want, but one wants more than the other. They go to war, and the better of the two survives and prospers. This is more true in a confrontation between civilized men and savages. The African, in his native state, is hardly better than a beast. In the wild, he is vicious and without morals. I have seen villages where men would eat their own tribe members."

William interrupted curiously. "Where is this?"

Baffled momentarily, Braganza waved away the question as being of no consequence. "Near the Gold Coast somewhere. I try to forget such places. Though, as I was saying, once the stronger of the two peoples captures his enemy, he may kill him, or he may spare his life. It is much more godly to spare the life of the weak." Carlos nodded confidently. "And what follows? By being spared, the life preserved is then indentured to the master, who has the authority to work the man, or execute him, as he might have done at first, having been shown to be the stronger of the two."

William briefly closed his eyes. "I understand. In that way, you *can* justify slavery."

"Yes!" Carlos exclaimed. "It is not bad, you see. You are sparing one's life and allowing him the freedom to work! And you are giving him the gift of civilization! Better food, better care, without the fear of wild beasts or brutal warfare. These are things that no man here would have had, if we did not bring them over." Carlos swept his arm toward the perimeter of the compound. Over a thousand slaves were engaged in the Braganza operation. "Remember also this: these men were in chains in Africa, captured by their enemies. Either man might have been the buyer or seller, but surely both were destined to be one or the other. These are the more fortunate savages."

"And is this not a huge expense?"

Braganza laughed. "One fine horse is worth one hundred Africans. It is the transportation that is the biggest problem."

A blacksmith was hammering leg irons around the ankles of several "fortunate savages." A similar hammer blow rang down on the shackle of truth that gripped William's thoughts: by shipping anything for Braganza, William was involved in the slave trade. And they had come at last to Braganza's grooming of William as a partner.

A year before he would have rejected the notion of being involved in the trade of human lives, but now he was not so set against it. To view it in Braganza's way shed a different light on slaving for William. Saving a man's life who was destined to be enslaved or killed no matter what was, in many ways, a service to the captured, William decided. At least, he attempted to believe it.

Clearing his throat confidently, the personable Carlos Braganza continued, "I must say, too, that Portugal is revolutionizing the industry by enforcing strict regulations for the treatment of . . . passengers . . . on our ships. We carry fewer per load, storage . . . cabin . . . areas are properly ventilated, and the vessel is thoroughly cleaned. There is no country that takes more care. Very humane, always."

Leading William toward an expansive, mudbrick industrial building, Carlos expounded. "Out there are the cane fields, and beyond them, the tobacco plantations. Much of the tobacco consumed on the Gold Coast is grown and harvested in Brazil. It is an interesting thing traders discovered during a drought year, when many crops had failed. Of the finest-quality tobacco, much was destroyed. It was the rugged, third-rate tobacco which survived to harvest." Carlos chuckled. "It is an amazing thing, I tell you! The tobacco was so dry it had to be mixed with molasses in order to keep it from crumbling. Traders feared African men would reject their produce, but to their surprise, the molasses gave the smoke a sweet taste, and to this day they will have nothing but!"

William shrugged. "A lesson in cultural taste?"

"Much more!" Braganza objected. "They call the tobacco *Soca,* making handsome bargains in slaves to obtain it. I ask you: Are not men worth more than tobacco?"

The two men stood in the high arched doorway of the dirt-floored room. William saw machines consisting of tall, vertically mounted gears: cane presses. There were ten of them on each side of the central aisle, each one cranked by teams of black slaves. One man at the front, where the upright wheels meshed, fed long shafts of sugarcane into the gnashing maw of the device. The whole contraption moaned as it spun, crushing and grinding the cane and spitting out sticky fluid into a pipe at the base.

"Efficient, these men," Braganza commented.

"Look at the effort they put into turning the mill. You would not find a light-skinned man in all of Brazil with such strength and stamina as these workers."

Braganza and William watched. "Nothing is wasted." The plantation owner pointed to the back of the enormous grinder. "The pulp you see spitting out the back of the drums is used as fuel. It burns hot indeed."

With a straw hat on his head, a black man wearing a canvas vest over a yellow shirt and tan trousers entered the room to supervise the progress of the work. Realizing the owner was present, the foreman let fall the short tails of a leather switch from under his arm. He lashed the men turning the crank and scolded them in an African tongue.

The slaves braced themselves lower and put their backs into it. The crushing drums moaned louder as they churned. About that same time the foreman lashed the one feeding the machine. He must not have heard the instruction over the monotonous hum, for he was startled by the whip. Forcing the last of a cane stalk into the machine and with one hand still near the grinding teeth, the slave lunged forward with fright.

Before anyone knew what had happened, the

African had practically disappeared into the machine. The gear drums came popping to a halt, grinding the man's arm all the way up to his chest. Braganza closed his eyes at the sight. William gasped and looked away from the atrocity.

The mangled slave screeched like a rabbit caught up in the razor-sharp talons of a hawk. The others ran to him, yanking on his opposite arm, trying to tear him free. The man wailed, and they let go, baffled and without another plan.

Weeping in pain, the man fell, hanging lifelessly by the mashed appendage. The foreman suddenly wielded a machete from his belt and hacked at the flesh and bone, severing the arm completely.

William gagged. The body on the ground hardly looked human. A few workers carried the unconscious man off but the rest returned to crushing cane. All had happened in mere seconds. Carlos led William away, returning in a fumbling but determined manner to how much better was the life of slaves in Brazil than at home in Africa. "We will save that man's life," he predicted. "But if he had been savaged by a lion or other wild beast, who would have saved him then? And see the discipline! The work was scarcely disrupted!"

A cocoa-skinned waitress swung a tray stacked with brimming tumblers high above the lively, lamp-lit, street-side hordes. William had been taken back to Rio to sample the entertainment of the teeming city. It had taken him several days to recover his appetite after the tragedy in the sugar mill, but now, with that horrific vision conveniently shoved aside, William's physical desires reasserted themselves. His mouth watered from the fragrant cooking smells that wafted by him as he swiveled from side to side in a wicker chair.

Seated at the table with him, Carlos Braganza fondled and cajoled a giggling woman whose arms encircled his neck. Gerald Fussel, absent on a trading voyage when William arrived in Brazil, but now returned in *Heart of Allegiance*, and deep in his cups, babbled on about the benefits of slavery. Michelle examined the ends of her hair and nails, expressing total, disgusted boredom. All around masses of the drunken and glutinous feasted and made merry with music, dancing, and debauchery. Four days of iniquity surrounded the feast of All Souls', second only to Carnival before Lent as a time of abandoned carousing.

William was hungry to taste the spicy food and quench his intense thirst by the rum that was being served. But his mind was also hungry for the wealth and success Braganza could bring him. Nor did his longings stop with the food, drink, money, or power; his masculine desires were craving Michelle. His eyes fell upon her and the low-slung neckline of her white, translucent cotton blouse. His imagination ran on. What would it hurt to get a little drunk? He licked his lips. What could be wrong with spending a little time with Michelle alone? *After all*, the voice inside his head argued, *you are sailing out again into a war. In an instant your life might be torn from you like that poor wretch's arm was from his body.*

Carlos continued to kiss and handle the woman on his lap until Michelle blurted, "That is enough, Carlos!"

It was clear Braganza was surprised to see her fury. The smile on his glowing face died like a snuffed candle. He helped the woman up from his knees. "I'm sorry, sweet," he said, pressing a coin into her hand.

Michelle glared furiously at the woman, then flung Braganza's drink all over her. "Get out of my sight!" she screamed, turning back to her father.

"It's not fun anymore! I am tired of this game!" Slamming her hands on the table, she stood and hurried away.

As William watched, stunned, he thought he heard a different voice whisper, *Be wary*. Suddenly the whole world crashed to a stop at his table. To him there was complete silence, as if he had been made deaf to everything but the whisper.

It came again. *Be vigilant, William.*

He spun round to see from whom it might have come. Gerald Fussel appeared positively frightened.

"Did you hear that voice?" William questioned, but Fussel paid no attention.

Braganza's face reddened further. He scrambled to explain. "She is jealous, you see. She imagines me only with her dead mother. I must go and console her." With that he hurried off in pursuit.

William's gaze fell quizzically on Fussel, who still acted afraid.

"Don't look at me," Fussel jabbered, "I've no idea what happened. She must be jealous like he said or something."

"How curious, though."

"What is?"

"She called him Carlos."

"Showing her scorn and disrespect?" Fussel offered.

The examination of this puzzle halted when a sailor from *Julia* sprinted up the street, dodging dancers and weaving through the crowd. "Mister Sutton! Mister Sutton! Captain Drake's apology, sir, but British ships have been spotted down the coast! They think they may be coming into port!"

William bounced to his feet. "Where is this?"

"Several miles south of the bay. You must hurry. The wind is against them, but if it turns . . ."

William faced Fussel and said sternly, "We must move both ships from port immediately. Though Brazil is neutral, the Royal Navy may blockade us for months, or treacherously take them."

Fussel, rousing from his drunkenness, slurred, "I will take *Allegiance* back to Charleston and await word from you there."

The two men set out in a hurried walk to the harbor, giving orders to a messenger to find Braganza and inform him of their urgent departure.

William's mind flashed to another matter that he had not yet had opportunity to quiz Fussel about. "What of my prize vessel Braganza acted as agent for?"

Fussel's eyes widened as if to furiously search the sky for answers. "It was recaptured."

"Recaptured!" William retorted. "How?! By whom?!"

"Right there in the port of Lisbon," Fussel continued nervously. "Some hours after you departed, Braganza informed me that two British frigates recognized it, violated the neutrality of Portugal, took it, and sailed it away to England."

"Impossible! That ship and cargo might have fetched over three hundred thousand dollars."

"It is a terrible shame."

William burned with frustration over the loss. For now, though, there were more immediate concerns as they headed down the steep gravel road toward the docks. If the frigates rounded into port before the American vessels got away, there would be two more ships to add to the list of the lost.

A flotilla of longboats rowed by an army of slaves towed the American Coastal Company ships out of harbor. Minutes later, their sails filling with the same breeze that would allow the British ships to finally approach from the south, *Julia* and *Allegiance* made good their escape.

As the *Julia* rocked out to sea, William thought of the unexplained warning and Michelle's odd behavior. It would be months before he saw her again. What might have happened if the curious interlude at the table had not occurred, or if the Royal Navy had not arrived? Was he disappointed or relieved?

Havana Harbor, November 1813. Fruitless cruises had yielded *Julia* no prizes, only a string of near-misses to British frigates. In port for replenishing supplies, William had not decided whether to join Braganza in the slave trade and its wealth yet; he was torn between sailing north to see his family and south to see Braganza and his daughter again. Apart from a pair of elderly seamen on anchor watch, the other *Julia* crewmen were ashore.

A mournful west wind at sunset was succeeded by a prickly night, loaded with unexplained noises and abruptly cut-off cries. William, tossing in his hammock aboard the *Julia*, was suspended in more than just air. Unable to fall to sleep, his disquieted thoughts jostled between worries about the emergency departure from Rio and concern for his family in Baltimore, whom William was anxious to see.

About midnight the uneasy stillness was ripped apart by a shouted argument. William scrambled topside to investigate. On a slave ship, not more than three hundred yards away, chaos was brewing. Fearful African voices chanted while chains beat out a devilish rhythm on metal grates.

Men wrestled with each other on deck. William could not see their faces.

"No!" screamed one. "I won't stay. I won't stay! Let me off this plague ship!"

"You have no choice! No one is allowed to land until after the quarantine is lifted."

"But we'll be dead! It's the cholera I tell you!"

"These orders cannot be changed. Stay back, or I shall have to shoot you!"

Simultaneously, two torch-lit longboats pulled alongside the slave ship's boarding ladder. Despite the shouted orders, crewmen began tumbling over the rails to escape the pestilence.

The officer tried to prevent the desertions but was overwhelmed by a wave of panic-stricken sailors. When a gun blasted, the body of a man was thrown backward over the rail of the slaver. Then came the cry, "The slaves! They're escaping!"

While William watched in horror, the rowers in the longboats methodically and calmly lit torches. One by one, they hurled them into the rigging and onto the deck, then paddled a distance away to rest on their oars and watch.

The sails ignited, illuminating the port in a grand orange funeral pyre. The light reflecting off low clouds caused the illusion of an upside-down bed of coals. Pieces of flaming canvas were lifted by the wind and carried toward the hovering inferno.

Breathing grew difficult for William as he was overwhelmed by the sense of evil in that place. Breaking wood and clanking metal gave way to splintering and the metallic creaks of nails being yanked from wood even as William found his own nails digging into his flesh.

Silhouettes of men writhed on the doomed ship. Women and children emerged from the hold, some shrieking hysterically in African dialects, others in Spanish or in English. The men beat at the flames, futilely, chaotically. Pieces of the rigging began to fall. A group of men, bearing chains and half-engulfed in flames, dived over the side, never to reappear. A section of mast fell on another swarming throng. Three of the men disappeared into the water, while three more were buried in the inferno, still attached to those crushed under the debris.

A woman held a baby by the neck like a rag doll, extended over the side, an arm's length away from the destruction. The frenzied screams increased. There was no one who would take the child, though the longboats were no more than a few oarstrokes distance. A wave of smoke swallowed the woman, all but her arm. Then a billow of flames. The grip, failing at last, relaxed. The infant fell, plunging into the turbid waters.

Feeling faint, William fell to his knees. The sight was worse than *any* battle he had seen. Just when he could watch no more, something drew his gaze.

"God, help! Set me free! Lord, set me free!" a slave's voice called in English over and over again. "I want to go home, Lord. Set me free!"

The whole ship exploded into a giant fireball. Flaming figures jetted into space, like human cinders popping across a demonic hearth. Then the ship burned to the waterline, and no more voices could be heard.

The smoldering hulk tilted, tipped, and capsized. Aside from creaking timber all was silent. Then the clunk and splash of oars told William that the escaping longboats neared the *Julia*. As the men peered up at him, he called to them with the only words he could speak. "It was more hideous than any sight I have ever seen."

A bearded man scowled at William. "It was a cursed loss of thousands of dollars of valuable slaves *and* a whole bloody ship. But necessary to keep the plague from spreading."

Fury welled up inside him. The vision of the woman pleading to save her child played over and over in his mind. He closed his eyes, reopened his eyes, but he could not stop the scene from replaying. The baby hung by its neck yards from rescue, and drowned in the abyss. Enraged, William roared at the men, "Babies and women! Children and babies and mothers and fathers died aboard that ship!"

William furiously scanned the decks for a weapon to hurl at the men. Seizing an eighteen-pound shot, he snatched it high above his head. The men cowered together. "You hell-bound creatures! What gives you the right to live?"

The officer trembled, then spoke. "They're only Negroes. Dead of the cholera soon anyway."

William snarled, "To hell with your ship and your money and your crew! To hell with you!!!" And he hurled the cannonball at them.

Diving out of the way, the slavers plunged into the water as the shot punctured their rowboat. A geyser of water rushed in; the men pawed to remain afloat.

Not satisfied with this action, William scrambled for another shot.

"He's crazy!" the sailors shouted. "Get away from him!" Swimming or paddling, the slavers made no further attempt to board the *Julia*.

William watched, shaking all over. His righteous fury broke into an intense pain that overwhelmed his body and his eyes. He collapsed on the deck. "Oh, God! God! Who could be the Lord of such evil men!" He remained that way, sobbing and wailing for hours.

CHAPTER 13

The tides of late November 1813 carried upon
them William Sutton and the war-weary crew
of the *Julia*. Upon the tides of his own worn emotions William brought his heart back home. It
seemed that the time away from Dora had allowed
him room to think about what she meant to him.
No longer was she merely his reliable, unexciting
wind, but instead a harbor of refuge he desperately
feared would be closed to him forever. Daring the
blockade, *Julia* sailed up the Chesapeake.

As William's ship docked, he peered down over
the edge to the gathering throng below. He eagerly
scanned the crowd for signs of Dora and found
only Grandfather Sutton and Billy.

Grabbing up Billy and putting an arm around

Grandfather Sutton's shoulder, he asked after Dora. The reply was exactly as he had expected.

"She's at the orphanage, Father," Billy replied with enthusiasm as he entangled himself around his father's neck.

"Ah. Well then, we shall go there at once."

Grandfather Sutton winked at William. Seeing the longing in his grandson's eye, he suggested, "Perhaps Billy and I will see the cargo unloaded and meet you at home for supper."

William, grateful for the opportunity to see his wife alone, grabbed up his duffel bag and a parcel of gifts for her and ran off to the converted parsonage.

William knocked, but no one came to the door. Cautiously, he pushed it open. The orphanage smelled of lye soap and boiled milk.

"Dora?" The sound of gurgling babies answered his inquiry.

Again. "Dora. Dora. It's me. William."

Footsteps echoed down the hall, and he heard Dora's voice calling over her shoulder with directions for the children to one of the nurses.

And then she was before him. Apron spattered with milk and all manner of baby smells. Wisps of hair sticking out from above her ears like outriggers on a canoe. Her face was flushed.

But William could not take his eyes off her. Wide with surprise at finding him there and startled at the gleam of tender love returned to his eyes, she stared back for a moment, then dropped her chin.

"Hello, William. I was unaware you had returned." Her eyes had betrayed a warmth in her soul that her words now edged in steely caution.

"Uh, yes." Unsteady, William merely sighed. "Dora . . ."

"I am needed in the back. Shall I see you at supper then?"

Her immediate dismissal hurt him more than he had anticipated, and he reasoned it was his fault for neglecting her so long. He did not want to leave, though, so he offered his help to wrangle more time with her.

"Dora, may I assist you? Perhaps there is a chore I can turn my hand at: changing, feeding . . ."

"Why, William, could that really be you?" she mocked. "Very well then. Out the back door to the side yard. You'll find the goat pen in need of mucking." She turned on her heel and left him to it.

An hour or so later, William returned, his chore done, and was immediately scolded by one of the nurses for tracking in muck on the bottom of his boots. He slipped them off and, in his stocking feet, padded through the various rooms, peering into each in search of Dora. He found her in the kitchen study doing the sums and figures for the week and catching up on correspondence to her sponsors. William rapped on the doorpost.

Dora drew a breath and said, "Come in, William."

She did not turn around but remained hunched over the desk as he entered and crossed the room to a chair behind her and a little to her left. The space did not permit them to sit side by side.

"I would like to discuss things with you, Dora," William offered as he glanced around the room. "I've been thinking. You don't have to answer; you don't have to look at me. But listen. Please."

Dora merely nodded and continued scratching away at the figures.

"I've watched your operation today. The children . . . they're beautiful. One of the nurses let me hold a baby. A boy. He smiled at me. All of them seem so . . ." He searched for the word. "Content. When I was in Brazil, I saw things that changed me. My heart. On a plantation there was a black man who was hurt . . . desperately injured . . . but his life was of less account than a penny's worth of sugar.

He wept and sobbed, but there was no mercy. That started the change, Dora. I see that now. And there was something else . . ." A tear swelled in his eye, and he brushed at it awkwardly as a man might shoo a fly.

Dora caught sight of this. "William? Are you all right?"

"Yes, I . . ." He stopped himself. No more running. No more lying. What had his ambition brought him? Busyness. A way of passing the time on the way to death. An abundance of worries and estrangement from his family. "No," he admitted, "I'm *not* all right. I saw a slave ship burned. Hundreds of people died horribly. There was a child, someone's beloved baby, one the mother wanted desperately to live. I . . . we have a son, and I want him to live and grow and be safe."

Now Dora was crying too. "Oh, William," she said, "when I could not give you a son, I thought I lost you. I lost myself. I needed to be needed, to feel valuable. I buried myself in this orphanage, to escape thinking of you, you see. But it never worked! I have thought of you constantly."

"Dora, Dora," William said on his knees, wiping her tears with his own wet hand, "we have a son. He does not have to be of our flesh to be of our hearts. He is ours to love. And so are these, your children. I'm sorry. I had no idea the need for your efforts until I saw *real* slavery. It may put chains on the lives of men, but it is the slavers who are changed into beasts. But you! You are the best of this earth. On the way up from the harbor people I did not know, black folk, greeted me and said, 'Lord bless your wife, Mister Sutton. God keep her.'" The flow of words finally slowed, and William said carefully, "Dora, I've come to ask your forgiveness for my selfish ways. I beg you, forgive me."

"William!" Dora leaped from the chair and clutched him, sobbing. She threw her arms around his neck and kissed him again and again. "William! William!" She said his name over and over and begged also for his forgiveness for her aloofness. Then words tumbled out. "William. My dear William. I've missed you, and I didn't think you would ever return to me. I worried about you, and we prayed for you every night. I wanted you, needed you to love me, but I didn't know how to reach you. Oh, William! Thank you."

After embracing for a time, William suggested they go home to the family for supper. Dora readily agreed and grabbed her cloak. With a farewell to the nurses, William and Dora Sutton headed toward home, the long way.

Dinner was a jubilant occasion in celebration of William's return. At its conclusion, William took Dora aside and asked sheepishly, "May I come to your bed tonight, Missus Sutton?"

Dora blushed. "Yes, Mister Sutton. I believe we have some catching up to do." They giggled a bit and then bid good night and stole away to get reacquainted.

Christmas 1813 in the Sutton household was warmer than it had been in several years, in spite of the winds that blew bitter and penetrating across the Chesapeake Bay. Even if the drafts in the house made things chilly, nothing could dampen the good cheer noted by all, except the prospect that, after the holidays, William would have to put to sea one more time. "The lone part of this Second War of Independence that is prospering," William said, "is the struggle at sea. I owe it to our adopted country to make one more cruise. Also, I know that Fussel and Braganza are up to something; I just don't know exactly what yet." There had been no word from Fussel or *Allegiance*.

William and Dora spent a lot of time together. It did not matter where they were, in the shipyard or at the orphanage; they held hands like young lovers. William was seen on several occasions wearing an apron and holding infants, and Dora was spotted gracing the decks of the Sutton ships from time to time.

William's departure in early January of 1814 was tearful for both with many hugs and kisses.

Dora, Billy, and baby Allie, in the care of a nurse, accompanied William aboard the ship for their farewell. Billy ran around below decks and above, pretending to set sail. Dora and William retreated to William's quarters for a last private moment.

"William, I don't want you to go. We've been given a second chance, and I'm . . . I'm afraid, William. I don't want to lose you."

"Why, Missus Sutton! Is that a tear in your eye? I won't be gone long, but it will, after this past month, seem an eternity."

"I'm fearful for you, William. I love you."

William drank long and deep of his wife's loving face, then moved to her. He wrapped her in his arms and kissed her forehead, her cheek, her neck, her lips. Tender and passionate, the distance between them had closed, and they held each other for a long time without talking.

The call was given to set sail, and William walked Dora to the gangplank. Again they embraced, and Billy sidled up next to his father. William hugged him, tousled his hair, and placed Dora's petite hand in Billy's youthful one.

One last kiss on the cheek, and William sent them ashore.

Dora waited to see the ship fade into the hazy reaches of the bay. As the last scrap of sail disappeared over the horizon sometime later, Dora wiped her eyes and cast her fond "I love you" on the wind.

Winter of the year 1814 was bleak in many senses of the word. The weather was especially harsh. Icy rain battered crops and killed livestock; prices soared and jobs dried up. The mood in Baltimore was foul as the British blockade dragged on.

Elsewhere, particularly in New England, people talked openly of a peace accord with Britain. Nantucket, the hulks of her once-proud fleet of merchant and whaling ships rotting at anchor, actually concluded a separate peace with England and declared herself to be neutral.

Dora and Angelique worked harder than ever to keep the orphanage heated and supplied, but shopkeepers who were previously generous turned indifferent or had nothing left to contribute. The rations for the children were diluted and then diluted again. Dora and Angelique made a pact to skip midday meals to leave more money for the babies' food, but when they discovered Billy and Cyrus doing the same thing, they put a stop to it.

Albert likewise grew thin. Despite his haranguing of citizens, the attitude in Baltimore was: Why should the British bother to attack us when they can starve us into submission?

Yet he labored on. Trenches were dug, and earthworks thrown up east of the city below Hampstead Hill. The whole town was divided into sectors, and, like ancient Jerusalem, every sector was given a space of wall to build. Boys as young as sixteen were enlisted in militia companies, often led by aged, tottering Revolutionary War veterans who had seen firsthand the disciplined firepower of the British redcoat.

Nor did Albert neglect the approaches by water. Gunboats were assigned to patrol the northwest branch of the harbor. Across its entrance scows were sunk to prevent warships from entering. The

point of land across from Fort McHenry was rein-
forced with cannon to prevent gunboats from
entering that way by hugging the shoreline.

The mouth of Bear Creek, a likely anchorage
for British troopships landing an invasion force,
Albert studied with particular attention. Too far
from Baltimore and too exposed to be successfully
defended, it was the perfect spot to adopt Robert
Fulton's suggestion: stores of gunpowder, fuses,
and watertight containers were stored in a secret
magazine. It remained merely to determine *how* to
use them.

Albert, to say nothing of Dora, often wondered
about William and his whereabouts, but after his
January departure, nothing had been heard. It was
as if he had again disappeared.

CHAPTER 14

Heart of Allegiance was nowhere to be seen. William scanned the busy waters of Charleston Harbor, expecting to meet up with Gerald Fussel. His instructions had been explicit and admitted no argument. But, William was later arriving at the rendezvous than he had planned.

He considered the possibility that *Allegiance* had been captured by the British, but felt surely he would have heard about it. With no sign of either ship or manager, William hoisted out a longboat and put in to shore.

Checking at the American Coastal Shipping Company office, William discovered that no logs had been updated since December. The premonition grew that something terrible had happened to his company's sloop. William wandered outside to think.

He stood on the platform overlooking the harbor, the same one from which Fussel had tempted his ambition and pride, for several minutes. Then a strangely familiar ship caught his eye. An English cargo vessel, two-masted; a hermaphrodite brig, half-square rigged, half fore-and-aft rigged, with a curiously long bowsprit.

Her crew prepped her for a sea passage. Men hung like monkeys from the rigging. High above the decks they swung hand over hand, back and forth, checking ropes for frays and blocks for fouling and cracks.

Nothing was out of the ordinary, except that William was sure he had seen the ship before. Then he gasped, "My prize!" in shocking revelation. It was the ship the *Julia* and crew had captured off the Azores.

He wasted no time in boarding it.

"Hello, sir," William announced, politely saluting a man who was bent over charts with a pair of dividers.

A whiskered gentleman he was, wearing an oiled rain hat despite the bright sun. His red skin was tight, etched with wrinkles. The fellow blinked at William, as if the thought of anyone interrupting him was too preposterous to be real.

"My name is William Sutton. I have an inquiry about this vessel."

The man, apparently an officer or sailing master from his map and compass, gawked at William, looked up at the sky, then returned to his work. "Let us see then. At forty-two north. Winds from the southeast . . . William Sutton?" he questioned. "American Coastal Shipping? Pleasure to meet you. Jack Fletcher. Your clipper-turned-privateer has made a name for herself." When at last Fletcher looked away from his charts, his eyes revealed a blankness that made William wonder if he had forgotten what he was doing.

"Yes, thank you. About this ship. Might you know where I can locate either the captain or owner?"

Fletcher grew oddly suspicious. "And why might you be wantin' that?"

William tried to think of a considerate way to ask where the ship had been purchased, but there was no easy way. "I am curious about the purchase of this vessel."

Fletcher cocked his head and retorted forcefully, "She's not for sale."

"No, no," William hastened to clarify. "I am interested in where the ship was last purchased."

"Oh yes, yes. It was . . ." Fletcher rolled his eyes wildly up. "Why would you be askin' that?"

This was a difficult chap, William realized. "*Julia* captured a ship very much like this one. It is British, is it not?"

Fletcher nodded. "Indeed."

"I figured her for that. And the reason why I trouble you is because the vessel was later recaptured by the British in the Bay of Lisbon, and I'm curious how she came to be in Charleston."

Fletcher's whiskers bristled like a cat's, and his cheeks swelled as he took offense at the insinuation. "The Bay of Lisbon, ha! This ship is not your prize. This ship was piloted up from Rio. Made a trip to Havana as a slaver, but they had bad luck . . . two thirds of the cargo died of the cholera. Sold her to me to cut their losses."

William was stunned. There was no doubt in his mind it was the same ship. "When was it purchased, Captain Fletcher?"

"Three or four months ago. Does that help you?" Fletcher widened his sagging eyelids to flash hazy yellow-and-green eyes at William.

Go slowly, William told himself. *Think it*

through. It is barely possible, but conceivable that the vessel could be taken by the Julia, *recaptured by the British, then captured again, used by someone in the slave trade, and sold again after. Surely a history such as this would be known.* "And are there logbooks for . . ."

"No! All logs were reported destroyed when the vessel was captured. Now, is there anything else I can help you with before you waste my day entirely?"

"Yes," William replied apologetically, with a close watch on the man's temper. "From whom was it purchased?"

"Get off my ship before I throw you off," Fletcher threatened. He picked up the pair of dividers and held them like a two-pronged dagger. "Comin' round askin' all kinds of questions. What are you tryin' to imply, Mister Sutton? And if you want to know anythin' else about the ship, I suggest you call on that slaver, Braganza. He's in Cuba, spendin' my money on his mistress and a broken-down sloop. Now get off!"

William made his way cautiously backward toward the gangplank.

"Braganza," William said in shock. "It *was* him. Or was it Fussel who lied to me?"

From the safety of the dock William called out, "What's the sloop called?"

"*Heart . . . Heart*, somethin'. But she's a bleedin' heart right enough. British frigate jumped her," Fletcher screeched, "with a full load of slaves! Bad luck all around!"

"With a load of slaves?" William started back toward the man, but was driven off by the divider that the man promptly hurled at him. It hissed past William's ear, missed a dockworker by inches, and embedded itself in a plank. "Slaves aboard my ship?" William repeated with a howl of dismay. "The cheating liar. He'll not use my ship for such devilish things if I can stop it."

William trotted to the longboat, rounded up what crew had landed, and headed out to the *Julia*.

"Where are we headed in such a hurry, Captain?"

"To Cuba," William replied in a low, determined voice. "We have a ship to intercept."

A gray, silhouetted strip of land was still in sight. The melting pink-and-tangerine sky over the island of Cuba may have been as clean and beautiful a sunset as ever a tropical sky painted, but

William did not notice. For several days he had walked the decks, shoulders hunched in determination to find the *Heart of Allegiance*. *Julia* examined Havana, poked into Guantánamo, explored sundry smaller, less-known harbors for the reportedly damaged *Allegiance*, all without success.

Increasingly there was grumbling among the crew. William was not only wasting time when he could be taking prizes, but he was endangering their mission since the British had surely heard that an American raider was lurking offshore.

William grew increasingly fearful that *Allegiance* had made her repairs and slipped away from him to an unknown destination. This apprehension drove him toward an insane rage. The motive for the obsessive pursuit came from three reasons: the vision of how cheap a slave's life was held by such men as Carlos Braganza, the atrocities slave owners could justify, and the fact that Gerald Fussel, the lying rat, had deceived him about the prize vessel. William wondered how many other deceptions there had been in his dealings with him.

Stalking about the stern railing with his hands clasped behind his back, William remembered another. Braganza had almost sent him into a trap by lying about the supplies and ammunition for the Spanish guerrilla fighters.

William was also furious at himself. The twin visions of Michelle's beauty and her father's offered wealth had almost totally destroyed his ability to see the truth, but he had gone down that path willingly.

He visualized again Braganza's smile and charismatic way. The merchant's humor was a facade for evil and greed, his winsome behavior a way to get what he wanted.

The scene of the harbor slave-ship holocaust returned. The heat from the flames . . . the screams . . .

The fire was fuel for his rage and the screams, those of Braganza. William could see himself punching the man in the face.

"Look alive on deck!" called a hand from the crow's nest. "Vessel off the starboard bow."

Sliding a telescope to his eye, William had trouble focusing because of the pounding of his heart. At length he replied, "We have them. It is the *Allegiance*." He stared at the ship, barely visible on the horizon. "All hands to general quarters! Prepare to engage the enemy!"

The shout bounced belowdeck, forward, and aft.

Men scurried to their places beside cannon and carronade. Cartridges of powder were hustled up from below. Buckets of seawater to fight fires lined the deck. Buckets of sand to absorb the spilled blood that made battle-footing treacherous were strewn across the planks.

"Captain Drake," William ordered, "we have the weather gauge. Prepare to engage that ship."

Drake did not question the command, though he knew that *Allegiance* was dear to William's heart. "Aye, sir. On this line our bowchasers will bear in no more than an hour."

"I do not wish to sink her," William said. "But she must not be allowed to escape. Is that clear?"

Minutes passed slowly as the *Julia* made a direct course for *Allegiance*. When the schooner's crew realized they were being stalked, they put the helm over, hoping to lie closer to the wind and outsail the privateer. But Captain Drake had anticipated such a maneuver, and the resulting course changes merely closed the gap faster.

"Sir," William's master gunner reported, "the starboard chaser will bear on the target. Do I have permission to try a ranging shot?"

His jaw set to preserve his control, William uttered the words, "Fire at your discretion."

Thirty seconds passed before the crash of an explosion disturbed the hiss of the otherwise-quiet seas. The round sailed over *Allegiance*'s yards, splashing down in a twenty-foot-high geyser on the far side. Incapable even of token resistance and clearly overhauled, the ship dropped sail and lay hove-to. Moments later a boarding party calmly took control of the ship.

Braganza smiled ingratiatingly as William climbed aboard. "William, my boy, it is good to see you. We thought you were a British blockade ship and had just recognized you when you fired. Was it not dangerous to fire a warning shot instead of a signal gun?"

The air aboard the previously clean and pure vessel smelled of human feces and rotting bodies. Gerald Fussel stood speechless. Michelle appeared from the captain's quarters to tuck herself beneath her father's arm.

"It is the proper greeting for thieves and slavers!" William retorted, his features swelling with rage at the continued deception. "I have never given my permission to use my vessel as a slave ship. I never would."

Braganza attempted to smooth his way out of the predicament. "But surely there has been a mis-

understanding between friends! Gerald thought
you would be pleased at the extraordinary profit.
And I, myself, understood you to be interested in
what I have achieved in Brazil. We are partners,
no?"

At that statement, William's fist flew through
the air exactly as he had imagined, striking Braganza dead in the nose. The man's body flew back
against some rigging, and he stumbled, falling over
a bucket.

"Carlos!" Michelle screamed, and the girl ran
to him, cursing at William in Portuguese.

Fussel also ran at William, attempting to grab
him. Captain Drake coolly stepped between them
and a second later a cocked pistol was leveled at
Fussel's temple.

"Chain these men below," William announced.
"And confine Miss Michelle to her quarters."

"But William," Braganza pleaded, staunching
the flow of blood from his nose with a handkerchief, "you are like my son."

"As much as Michelle is your daughter."

Michelle's face took on a frightened, hunted
look. "He made me . . ."

"Shut up, you fool!" Braganza hissed.

"I never wanted to hurt you, Senhor William,"

Michelle continued. She flung herself at William, grabbing him around the knees.

William shook her off with disgust. "On second thought," he said, "confine Mister Braganza's mistress belowdecks as well."

As she struggled to fight loose of the sailors who pinioned her, she again cursed loudly in Portuguese.

It did not matter to William if she hated him. Michelle, her spoiled, pouting deviousness, had become more revolting to him than the others. She made him feel unclean. He shuddered at the thought of what he had nearly done, what he had almost lost. "Take them below."

William addressed the rest of the crew aboard *Allegiance*. "As for the rest of you, many of whom I know, you will not be arrested or held accountable for the actions of these men, as long as you continue to comply with my orders."

The tense atmosphere relaxed.

The *Allegiance*'s sailing master stepped forward. "Where to, Mister Sutton?"

William looked around at the men. All eyes waited for him. He gazed down through the grates where the slaves were huddled in chains, then back to the crew. "Is there an interpreter aboard?"

"I am here, sir." A slender man stepped forward.

"Ask these men if they would like to return home."

Gasps and chatter filled the air, while the man popped and grunted in an African tongue. Below the deck grating one large, muscular fellow was pushed forward as spokesman. Grasping the bars, he spoke through the interpreter.

"Home, sir?"

William clarified, "To Africa, tell him."

The man stared back at him. At first William was unsure if the man understood. Then a tear fell from the man's eyes, and William knew the answer before the man spoke again.

The interpreter relayed the reply. "He said, 'If there is a God as white men say, let you tell the truth and set him free.'"

William cleared his throat, searched the solemn faces, and replied, "Give him my word. There is a God, and he shall be set free."

The hands cheered. Never before had they seen a man give up so much wealth. But if William gave his word, they knew it was as good as gold.

The celebration was halted by a desperate shout.

"There!" a lookout's voice shouted. "South!

Less than a mile off!" he cried. "Two British frigates approaching!"

William spun round to see and realized they were closer than that. "All hands to make sail!"

Men scrambled back over the side. Cannons were run out and sails sheeted home, but William knew their efforts were hopeless. The frigates were on the same wind that had allowed *Julia* to capture *Allegiance* with such ease. They were too mightily armed to outfight and too close to outrun.

William ordered *Julia* to fire a starboard broadside aimed high at the leading frigate, in the hope of dismasting her with a lucky shot and buying time to flee the remaining challenger. The three-hundred-weight of iron sliced across the waves, but apart from a pair of shotholes, no other damage could be seen.

The fire that replied was murderous.

Twice that weight of metal savaged *Julia*'s decks, killing Captain Drake and three others, wounding six more and dismounting two of the starboard guns.

It was madness to continue to fight.

The colors of both American vessels were hauled down, and a second surrender took place within an hour of the first.

Failure slammed into William harder than the impact of the cannonballs. His ships were lost, his part of the war sacrificed, his friends killed, and who knew what would now become of his promise to the slaves? While he had been pursuing his own obsession, he should have been keeping watch. How could he have done such a stupid, stupid thing? A wave of defeat from his previous mistakes crashed down on him at once. It was almost more than he could bear.

The boarding party clambered aboard. Men with muskets scattered to the corners of the ship. William stepped forward.

A clean, good-looking, middle-aged man in the uniform of a Royal Navy captain marched boldly toward him. "Where is the man in charge of this vessel?"

"I am here, sir," William replied dispiritedly.

"There is no need to try and hide your identity," the admiral proclaimed. "You are the notorious pirate, Sutton. Traitor to England and . . ." The officer sniffed the tainted air. "Involved in illegal trade in slaves as well, I'll be bound. Three capital crimes, and only one neck for them all. What bad luck for you," he added. "Today was our last day of searching for you. We are ordered north."

"We operate a duly authorized letter of marque," William said warily. "We are not pirates. As for the slaves, that is what I came here to remedy."

The admiral snorted. "Some men will say anything to save their lives, eh, Sutton? I'd hang you right away if I did not have strict orders to return you to England. And that will be after we crush your foolish President Madison and your upstart republic." Turning abruptly, the admiral turned to his flag lieutenant and ordered, "Mister Freed, signal to *Hyperion*: Keep station to windward and astern of the two prizes while we take the lead. Set course for Chesapeake Bay."

"Chesapeake!" William mouthed as he was hustled below and chained. The last shock was complete. "This is the invasion, come at last. Dora's there, and Billy." Frustration made him tug at his bonds and scream. "Let me go!"

A redcoated guard smacked the bulkhead beside William's ear with a belaying pin. "You there. Be quiet."

"No!" screamed William, feeling as though he were losing his mind. "Let me free from here."

"Shut yer gob, Yank!" ordered the man. William lunged at him. The young soldier smashed the wooden peg into William's head. The world dimmed as William fell to the floor.

March 9, 1814, dawned sunny and warm with fresh hints of spring on the breeze.

Dora rose at her customary early hour but was not feeling quite herself. She went down to breakfast and discovered that absolutely everything brought before her made her uncomfortably near to vomiting. Finally she managed a piece of dry toast and some weak tea.

Grandfather Sutton frowned his concern, but the now strong-willed Dora brushed it off with a wave of her hand.

"I'm sure it's nothing. A last-season ague or a touch of *la grippe*. Exhaustion, perhaps. I'll be fine as soon as I get to work and get my mind off it."

But she was not well and that became painfully clear as she stood up from the table. Her face paled and despite her effort at straightening up, she gave an inescapable squeak. Grasping her side, Dora crumpled to the floor in a wave of nausea and light-headedness.

Grandfather Sutton leaped from the table in an

effort to catch her, upsetting the table settings and scattering cups and teakettle, marmalade pots and scrapple.

Grandfather Sutton dabbed his napkin in a glass of water and laved her temples to bring Dora around, while calling for someone to fetch the doctor immediately.

He managed to carry her upstairs to her bed and remained there with her until the doctor arrived three-quarters of an hour later.

Dr. Polson, a short man with tufts of white hair and a perpetual smile that dimmed the sun, was fond of giving robust and enthusiastic embraces to all but his adult male patients. Babies were his favorite clients.

As soon as he arrived, he ushered Grandfather Sutton from the room and said, "I'll just be a few minutes with her and then you can return." He closed the door.

Grandfather Sutton paced the floor outside Dora's room.

Angelique whisked into the hall a short while later, greeted Grandfather Sutton, and disappeared into the room with the doctor and Dora.

Muted voices came from beyond his range of hearing. They sounded like concerned questions with Dora's soft voice replying. Then Dr. Polson laughed heartily, and the door was flung wide. The good-natured physician beckoned Grandfather Sutton to enter.

"Well, Randolph. Nothing serious, it seems, or rather, serious but not solemn. In fact, quite the opposite I should think. Shall I tell him, young lady? Or would you like the honors?"

Dora nodded her assent and then smiled tenderly at Grandfather Sutton. "I am pregnant again. About three months."

Grandfather Sutton's eyes brimmed with joy, and he exultantly clapped Dr. Polson on the back. He walked over to Dora's bedside, bending low to kiss her forehead and stroke her hair. Then he and Dr. Polson left the room, jabbering on about the wonderful news.

Dora watched them go and reached for Angelique's hand.

"Come sit with me a while, Angelique."

Angelique did as she was asked but said nothing. She held Dora's hand, and for a long time they were silent. Dora stared up at the curlicues of the sculpted-plaster ceiling. When she finally spoke, her voice quivered with uncertainty.

"Oh Angelique, I want to be happy about this.

I want to allow myself to believe it could really happen. But what if . . . what if I can't . . ." She could not finish the thought, so Angelique finished it for her.

"*Cherie,* we must think positively about this. God has again allowed you to conceive. There is a plan. Always a plan, no? This will work, and you will bring a new life into this world."

"And what of William? He's again at sea, and who knows if I shall see him again? What if he never sees, or has the opportunity to hold, or even *know* about this child?"

Angelique let out a long breath as she contemplated Dora's doubts and fears. Sensing there was no appropriate answer, she scooted Dora over in bed and joined her. Holding Dora's head against her breast, Angelique soothed her sister-in-law's quaking soul and encouraged her to let her tears cleanse her of anxiety.

It was not long before Dora was ready to think of baby things, nurseries, and all things small and dainty.

Then suddenly she sat up in bed, exclaiming, "Oh! And what of the orphanage? I've much to do! I can't be here."

"*Mon Dieu!* Dora! You are pregnant. Enjoy this

time, and I will see to the orphanage. You must not, eh, how do you say . . . do it over? No, overdo it! You must be still and allow this life to cling to you and you to it. Now, lie down."

As soon as Dora was situated again and had resigned herself to being in bed for a while, Angelique bustled out of the room to see to the care of the orphanage on behalf of her dear sister and friend.

CHAPTER 15

The Second War of Independence, or as the disgruntled citizens of Baltimore currently called it, "Mr. Madison's War," dragged on into its third year. In July eight thousand Americans tried again to invade Canada . . . and failed. The British captured eastern Maine, opening a direct land route into New England, and ten thousand redcoats were said to be on the march from Montreal.

Word finally reached Baltimore that William had been captured—wounded and captured, it was said—but nothing further. It was not known whether he was alive or dead, a prisoner in the British fleet patrolling outside Chesapeake Bay or already back in England awaiting trial for treason. The Sutton family prayed for his deliverance, for his safety, and for word about both.

In the dismal heat and humidity of the last week of Baltimore August, Dora tottered painfully on swollen feet back and forth through the rooms in the orphanage. Her belly swollen with impending delivery, Dora could scarcely walk, and bending over to retrieve a dropped diaper pin was out of the question.

While things inside the orphanage remained well-ordered, the rest of Baltimore was scurrying about with the threat of war.

Daily the townspeople fled in droves, abandoning all but the essential items for their survival.

The British were coming again, and this time there would be no General Washington to gather the tangled skein of command.

One day, while Angelique was out gathering supplies for the orphanage, she was roused to frustration by comments that the darkies should be left to starve. "There won't be enough food for us if this blockade lasts much longer," the speaker complained. "And when we take to the roads I say let the blacks tend for themselves, instead of letting uppity Negroes take provender out of the mouths of white folk."

She wheeled around to see who was making such horrific remarks only to find it was a deacon of the church.

The next day, about noon, a rock was thrown through a window at the orphanage. Shouts and curses came from outside. As Dora herded children and nurses with infants into a back room, Angelique peered around jagged shards of glass to see what was happening. Her hand flew to her mouth as she recognized Quince and Saul, her two assailants from the goat pen. Saul was bellowing, and a crowd gathered to listen.

"They have food!" he yelled, pointing toward the orphanage. "They have a secret store of food, bought by New England abolitionists!" This brought a discontented murmur from the crowd. "It's a plot, just like those New Englanders have sold out to the British! The Yankees want us to starve. There's a plot for slaves to rise up and take over this town, and I tell you, the headquarters of that plot is right there!"

"What'll we do?" asked Quince, ever the good shill.

"Burn 'em out!" Saul roared. "Take their abolitionist food and gold and burn the place down!"

"Yeah!" agreed a bystander. "Why should nigger babies have food and us go hungry?"

"And work!" another added. "I ain't had more'n two days labor in months. It's them free blacks that done it. The last thing we need is more of them!"

"Who's with me?" Saul demanded.

Angelique shrank back from the window, wondering if there was time to run for the militia company that was drilling below the brow of the hill . . . then noted that two in the mob wore the crossed white belts of militiamen.

"Oh, God," she prayed out loud. "Send us deliverance for the children's sake." She would lead them out the back. The orphanage and what they had built would be lost, but the children would be saved.

Another rock crashed through a window, and another battered into the front door. Any moment the preliminary buildup of rage would finish, and the rush to destroy would follow.

Then, miraculously, there was a clatter of hooves on the road outside and panicked calls as a hurrying horseman scattered the crowd. The rider was shouting something. What was it?

"The British are marching on Washington!" Angelique heard. "Men are needed to go to the defense! Militiamen, report to your companies at once!" Then the horseman galloped away to spread the alarm.

"Let's finish this business first," Angelique heard Saul yell. "Besides, let those fools in Washington fend for themselves."

Angelique was so incensed at this display of cowardice and prejudice that she flung open the door and cried, "Where have all the men gone? Is there no one left to fight the real enemy, or are you all cowards?"

Saul tried to drown out her words with curses, but the crowd listened to what she said. "Can you doubt the English will come here next? Is this soil not our own? *Oui!* And why should we flee this hard-won land? Why are we giving it over to British tyranny? Can you simply walk away from what is rightfully yours? No! This is my home. I am an American, and those who threaten my homeland threaten me. The enemies of this place are *my* enemies. I will not leave. *Mon Dieu!* You people do not know how to see the real enemies in your midst." She extended a slender, accusatory finger toward Saul and Quince. "Who is aided if you are prevented from marching toward Washington? Who but the British?"

"Say, that's right," an onlooker assented, changing his mind. "And these two don't look like they missed many meals, either!"

The crowd was still murmuring, but the gathering's opinion had swung clearly in Angelique's favor. Those who wanted to fight the British outnumbered the rest, and Saul and Quince fled.

Angelique called for the men to fight the Second War of Independence, and soon there were men waving their arms high in the air to sign up for this makeshift army. The men of Baltimore would fight. Washington would not fall to British hands without a struggle. Baltimore would be defended, if need be, with street-to-street barricades like those of Paris. Angelique demanded it be so.

The prison ship *Cerberus* was a floating dungeon, complete with rats, overflowing bilges, moldy crusts of bread, and drinking water containing all manner of swimming vermin. William had been in her hold for four months.

After his capture he had first been confined for over a month belowdecks on the frigate *Imperious*. That incarceration, though harsh, was nothing compared to his present circumstances. William had reached his present cesspool of a cell by trying to escape from *Imperious*. Remembering Captain Shraider's story, William knocked down a guard and attempted to jump over the rail and swim for shore when two British tars seized him and dragged him backward.

After a flogging, William was remanded to the custody of the newly appointed chief of naval prisoners: former lieutenant and now captain, Benton Hazzard. Hazzard's smirk was even harder for William to swallow than the drinking water. "I told your brother we would meet again, Sutton," Hazzard said, sneering. "I swore to myself that I would personally have the pleasure of putting the rope around your neck, and this situation is close enough!"

There was one other prisoner enchained on the lowest deck of *Cerberus*. His back crisscrossed with so many whip marks that it resembled a turtle's shell, George Washington Canfield said he had not seen the sun in many months, nor did he expect to again.

"You haven't been down here since you were pressed in '07, have you?" William asked, aghast.

"No, sir," Canfield explained. "Served my time in the *Leopard;* other ships too. Took my share of floggin's, but that don't signify. Fought the French and did my part. Was when my ship sailed here to go to war with America that I came to grief. 'Serve that gun, Canfield,' the English told me. 'No, sir,' I said. 'Not gonna fire on my American flag.' Don't know why they haven't hung me yet. Get around to it most any day, I expect."

"Me too," William noted. "Me too."

Though Albert was in Washington, he was not participating in defense. But then, no one was. He was helping to rescue a pair of six-pound cannons, abandoned by their crews in front of the President's House. President Madison himself had fled the city. It was thought that the British would arrive any time.

There had been a defensive line at Bladensburg, ten miles northeast of the capital. It had been a good position: six thousand men on a hill commanding the eastern branch of the Potomac River, cannon to cover the river crossing, plenty of time to prepare.

Then the British arrived. After a brief skirmish and some long-range cannonfire by the Americans, the redcoats unleashed a secret weapon: Congreve rockets. These uncontrollable, hissing, fizzing, exploding implements of war did little actual damage, but terrified the barely trained militiamen.

A British charge across the bridge was decimated by a salvo of guns, but before the artillery could reload, the redcoats marched across the river in force and attacked the hill.

The defenders took one last look at the British bayonets glittering in the sun and took to their heels. Most did not stop running before reaching Washington.

So here was Albert, having joined an infantry regiment in a hillside orchard only to see his comrades race away at almost the first volley. Here was Albert, trying feverishly to save what could be saved from the relentlessly advancing British.

Albert collared a pair of retreating infantrymen. "Haul me this cannon out to the west," he demanded.

"And who do you think you are?" one of them returned. "Lafayette?"

"*Diable!*" Albert retorted, whipping a pistol out of his belt. "You will think I am the devil if you do not do as I say. Now drag that gun to safety!"

The president's doorman, French-born Jean Pierre Sioussa, heard Albert's accent and gestured for him to come into the mansion. "We need your assistance," he said.

Wondering whether this call was for an especially dangerous mission, or to remove important documents, Albert was led, not to an office, but to the dining room. "We cannot allow it to fall into British hands," Sioussa said, gesturing at the portrait of George Washington hanging on the west wall. "It is screwed in too tightly."

Nearly exploding with laughter at the ludicrous situation, Albert controlled himself when the president's wife entered the room. "Please, sir," Dolley Madison implored. "It would shame me terribly if the British captured it."

Inclining his head chivalrously, Albert asked for an ax. Perching precariously atop a ladder, he hacked apart the frame of the picture and lowered the canvas to the floor.

Two hours later, from atop a hill west of Washington, Albert once again stopped to rest and look back over the scene of the latest retreat. What he saw appalled him: the Navy Yard was burning, Tomlinson's Hotel was ablaze, smoke poured from the Capitol building, and finally, the President's House was torched.

"*Sacre bleu!*" Albert said under his breath. "What they do here, they will repeat in Baltimore! We must keep them even from entering it; I must go!"

He rode off through a shattering thunderstorm. As if the day had not had rockets enough and volleys of musket fire in plenty, the night made up for any lack with lightning bursts and torrents of rain.

The orange glow in the sky above the destruction of Washington was visible from Baltimore, forty miles away. Thus, visual confirmation of the devastation reached Dora and Angelique long before Albert's return, but at the same time as the news of William's fate.

There was a late-night knock at the door of the orphanage.

Angelique opened it to find Georgetown attorney Scott Key, his cape swirling about him in the gale. "Good evening, ma'am," he said with a bow. "But it is not a good evening, as I'm sure you are aware. I apologize for calling so late, but I have news of especial import to Missus Dora Sutton. May I come in?"

Key was shown into the parlor, and Angelique replaced Dora in the rocking chair where she was struggling to find room around her pregnant stomach for a pair of fractious, teeth-cutting children.

"Courage, *cherie*!" Angelique urged. "There is a man here. Mister Key, you remember? He says he has news for you."

Her heart beating in her throat, Dora greeted the lawyer. "Is it about my husband, Mister Key?" she asked with a quaver in her voice.

"He is alive, ma'am!" Key hastened to say, easing Dora into a chair. "I'm sorry to have frightened you. He is aboard a British prison ship, but he is alive."

"Thank you, oh, thank you!" Dora gushed, clasping the jumping baby in her womb with both hands. "God be praised! He doesn't even know he's going to be a father."

Key stood gravely, twisting his hat in his hands. "There is more," he said at last.

"Yes?" Dora said, her spirits plummeting again as fast as they had risen. "Where is he? Can I see him?"

"He is awaiting the conclusion of the present campaign before being returned to England . . . where he is under sentence of death for treason."

Dora swooned away.

CHAPTER 16

───⁂───

On Sunday, September 11, 1814, the combined British fleet of warships and troop transports anchored at the point where the Patapsco River flows into Chesapeake Bay. The attack on Baltimore was ready to begin. Three cannons booming in succession warned the citizens the assault was imminent, but the signal was largely unnecessary, since almost the entire population was atop Hampstead Hill watching the armada anchor.

Albert, true to his calling as master of defenses for the city, did not spend any time gawking at the harbor. There were more trenches to be dug, cartridges to be readied, cannonballs to be trundled by wheelbarrow to the waiting guns.

There was also the matter of the torpedoes.

The larger vessels in British Admiral Cochrane's

force blockaded the river mouth, about three miles from Fort McHenry. Located as they were in the center of the channel, there was no chance of approaching them.

But the troop transports were another matter.

From a score of volunteers at American Coastal Shipping, he selected a handful of trustworthy men to carry out a midnight raid. A flaming fire ship would put out from concealment and make directly for the fleet, but this was merely a diversion. The true threat would come from boatloads of explosives towed from the opposite direction. It was a doubtful plan at best. There was small chance of destroying one of the ships, and less chance that more than one attack could be carried out after the first explosion, but Albert hoped the stratagem would at least give the British pause, make them worry about what was happening behind their lines, cause them to draw back.

Anything to keep them out of Baltimore.

Then, in one of those quirks of fate, Albert's plan lost any hope of success. Bear Creek, where Albert had guessed the transports would anchor, was unoccupied. But the ships containing the red-coated soldiers actually moored down the channel, near North Point. There, in the shelter of Old Roads Bay, they would unload the men who would march on Baltimore.

Albert had recently returned to his position atop Hampstead Hill when Scott Key approached him. "I have just received permission to visit Admiral Cochrane aboard the frigate *Surprize*. I am going there to arrange a prisoner exchange. I thought perhaps . . ."

There was no need for Key to finish. Albert leaped at the chance to intercede on behalf of his brother.

Racing homeward, Albert constructed a plan. Drawing Angelique aside from Dora's confinement, he kissed her passionately. After hugging his children, he explained there was a chance to save William's life. He would try to change places with his twin brother and let William return to safety. If the imposture could be carried out, Albert could later prove his actual identity; he could not be regarded as a traitor to England. He did not *think* they would hang him for protecting his brother. He kissed them again, and told Angelique he did not know when he would see her next.

Hugging her ferociously, she said he was the

best man she had ever met or would ever meet, then told him, "Go! Waste no time. For Dora's sake, go!"

The flag-of-truce sloop carried the prisoner-exchange committee down channel to meet the British admiral. His vessel lay anchored alongside the prison ships.

Once aboard, two unexpected and unpleasant things happened: the British officers refused to speak with Albert about William or allow him to see his brother on the *Cerberus*. The second surprise was that while Cochrane would honor the flag of truce, he was about to launch his attack; he would not allow Scott Key or Albert to return to Baltimore.

At three in the morning on September 12, the British army was floated ashore from their transport craft. At seven they were on the march toward Baltimore. By three in the afternoon two things of significance had happened: the redcoats had pushed the Americans out of defensive positions east of Baltimore, opening the route to attack the city on the following day. The other important occurrence was the death of the commanding

British general, Robert Ross, felled by American sharpshooters.

The news of his comrade's death enflamed Admiral Cochrane. Baltimore would not be spared any ravages if it did not surrender at once. He would treat it more harshly than Washington. So the next day the army advanced to within sight of the trenches lining Hampstead Hill.

An assault on the defenses on Hampstead Hill was ordered by Ross's replacement, Colonel Arthur Brooke, for 3:00 A.M. the following morning. Brooke's plan included an all-out bombardment of Fort McHenry by the navy rocket and bomb ships, so as to divert attention from his attack and draw defenders away.

Accordingly, all day long on the thirteenth and past midnight on the fourteenth, Cochrane's mortars lobbed shells over the fort's thirty by forty-two foot flag.

Within the heart of the town, a bomb of another sort was detonating. Dora, Angelique, and the nurses were busying themselves, hanging blankets over windows to prevent them from shattering from the concussions of the British invasion when it happened: Dora stretched to fasten a corner of one of the blankets and overextended herself. A piercing pain wracked her entire body, throwing her to the floor.

When the pain subsided, she tried to right herself. Angelique struggled to help her to her feet. Dora, trembling under the weight of her pregnancy and limping toward a chair, was suddenly covered in a gush of fluid as her water broke.

Albert watched flights of rockets scream toward Fort McHenry. The sky was darkened from the fumes and dust of explosions. Bomb vessels edged closer, lobbing mortar shells that burst over the bastion, raining red-hot shards of jagged metal on the defenders, until driven back in turn by cannonfire from the fort.

In the afternoon the prison ships anchored near Albert's temporary lodging became active. Up-anchoring, they hoisted sails for steerageway as the incoming tide carried them north.

Stopping a passing guard, Albert asked what was happening.

The guard peered at him suspiciously, then shrugged. "No 'arm in tellin' you that," he allowed.

"We expect a lot of your blokes to come back as prisoners from the attack. Admiral wants them ships moved closer to the fight so as to receive 'em without muckin' up things 'ere."

Inwardly quaking, Albert asked, "Can you tell me where they will be?"

"I dunno," the guard replied. "Place called *Bear Creek*, or summat like that."

The distant crump of exploding bombs was perfectly timed with each contraction. It seemed the arrival of the new Sutton baby was marching to the heart-thumping percussion going down at the bay.

Crump. Boom! Crump. Boom!

Breathe. Push! Breathe. Push!

Progress was slow.

Billy and Grandfather Sutton, along with Angelique's children, were sentenced to play with the babies while all the adult females saw to Dora. Occasionally one would carry a progress report to the exiles, only to vanish back to the great mystery of womanhood shortly after.

CHAPTER 17

Night fell, but there was no lessening of explosions. Rockets traced spirals of reddish flames, or pinwheeled before detonating in brilliant light. Watching, Albert caught glimpses of the immense flag waving over the fort. McHenry's guns roared back their own challenges to any British ships foolish enough to come within range.

Inside Albert felt paralyzed. Surely the torpedo attack would not take place at all. His men had received no word from him in two days.

Besides, even if they launched the assault, what were the odds they would pick the vessel on which William was confined? Surely that could not happen.

Could it?

Should he stop it from happening by warning the British?

But how could Albert tell a British officer what was afoot without getting his men killed, even if he cared nothing of putting his own head in a noose?

If his plan to free William had worked, then the use of the torpedo would only have endangered his own life and not his brother's. Now there was nothing to be done but watch and pray.

Dora's labor intensified, with no medicine to ease her pain. The air, rank with the odors of sulfur and death, choked her, making it difficult to push. Angelique and the nurses coaxed her gently at times, and at other times spoke harshly so she would not give up.

The pictures hung crazily crooked on the walls. Dora wondered if she were delirious, since they seemed to jump to different slants every time she closed her eyes.

She opened her mouth to ask Angelique about it, but was immediately seized by another violent contraction.

"What do you 'spose is happenin'?" George Washington Canfield asked William.

"Impossible to tell," William said. "Nobody tells us anything. First I thought they were moving us out of harm's way. Then, when the explosions got louder, I wondered if we were going right up to the fight. Now, I don't know. We're anchored again and swinging with the tide. One thing's for sure, they haven't won yet, or they would not still be throwing shot."

"Go for it, Balt'Mer!" Canfield urged. "Pour it to 'em. I expects you to do me proud. What was that?"

The last question was occasioned by a thump against the hull on the opposite side of the ship. Then overhead came the sound of running feet and a ragged rattle of musketry.

"Could it be a rescue?" William wondered. "Stay alert, George. Maybe we have friends nearby."

Outside Baltimore men hung from tree branches like obscene ornaments, resting where exploding shells propelled them.

Lifeless forms floated in Chesapeake Bay, dumped unceremoniously overboard after being killed at their action stations.

The British Colonel Brooke drew up his plans,

his men, sent orders and counterorders to his regimental commanders . . . and did nothing to launch the assault on Hampstead Hill.

A giant hand seized the *Cerberus*. Lifted abruptly into the air, its keel broken in two, the prison ship settled on its side in the Chesapeake. William Sutton and George Washington Canfield were in a part of the ship that held air, but for how long? And they were still shackled to the bench in total darkness.

"Don't worry," Canfield urged, rattling his chains in a purposeful fashion. "I'm a carpenter. Me and wood, we got an understandin'. I've been whittlin' away with a little bittie file for most a month."

There was the sound like a pistol shot as he cracked the remaining scrap of wood to which his chains were bolted. Moments later he released William.

Water was swirling into the hull, rising higher all the time. "That's our way out," Canfield said, slapping the surface. "I saw the crack in the hull before she settled. We can swim out that way."

"Swim? How?" William asked with an edge of panic. "We have chains on our wrists."

"That ain't nothin'," Canfield returned. "Just you loop your arms over my head. I swim good enough for two. I'll be your deliverance, like. Now, deep breath, and here we go."

Five o'clock in the morning.

The rolling thunder had nearly ceased. The occasional reports of small arms continued, but the constant drumming of mortar shells ceased, at least for a time.

One last push and a steady wail from an infant longing to return to the womb rewarded Dora's efforts. Whisked away to be cleaned and wrapped, the baby girl was returned to her mother's arms almost before Dora was aware she had succeeded.

At the nurse's gentle prodding, Dora held the infant to her breast to offer nourishment and comfort. She wanted to watch the baby nurse but was overcome with exhaustion. She collapsed back against the folded blankets behind her head and shoulders.

When the newborn had her fill, she sighed with contentment and nuzzled into her mother's bosom for a nap.

With a sigh of her own Dora murmured,

"William . . . we did it. Julia Emily Sutton. Praise God. Both our mothers are smiling from heaven."

To which those present added a fervent amen.

Dora's arms were empty no longer. The Lord had crowned her embrace of unwanted children with one of her very own.

Colonel Brooke gave up the assault. The frustrated redcoats grumbled about the lack of courage in their replacement commander but obeyed and marched back to the transport ships.

Onboard the truce ship, Albert and Francis Scott Key watched anxiously for dawn to break. The stoppage of the shelling was ominous. It could mean the end of the defense of Baltimore with the lowering of Fort McHenry's flag.

Then, through gray light hung thickly with smoke, the distant outline appeared; the Stars and Stripes still waved above the citadel; the defense had held. Scott Key muttered lines of doggerel; images of "bombs bursting in air."

Albert, heartsick ever since the eruption and giant crash that came from the direction of Bear Creek inlet, prayed and prayed. He wondered if his brother was dead, then realized that if his plan to

304

change places with William had succeeded, he would have been the one caught in the destruction.

A half-mile away, dripping and covered in mud, William Sutton and George Washington Canfield emerged from hiding at the edge of the waters of the Chesapeake.

Lifting his hands heavenward, Canfield spoke for both men. "Thank you, Lawd!" he said passionately. "We're free!"

HISTORICAL EPILOGUE

William Sutton was indeed fortunate to escape being returned to England for trial. Twenty-three other naturalized American citizens (a change of nationality never recognized by Britain) were kept incarcerated in Dartmoor Prison, under sentence of death for treason, even after the war's end. On April 6, 1815, these prisoners rioted. Five were killed.

What we now refer to as the war of 1812 and what was then called the *Second War of Independence* is arguably the most unnecessary conflict ever fought, since many of the substantial matters of disagreement were resolved before war was declared. A similar tragedy of that era of slow communication led to an ironically fitting conclusion: the Battle of New Orleans, a resounding victory for

American forces under the leadership of future president Andrew Jackson, was fought on January 8, 1815, two weeks *after* the Treaty of Ghent was signed.

One result of the war was to fill the forty-year-old United States with pride, and secure her position as a sovereign nation, able to assert herself in the wider world.

What the conflict *did not* settle were the questions of slavery and the rights of black citizens. Those lingering wounds would fester for another forty-some years and then erupt into bloody civil war, with repercussions that continue to haunt us down to our present day.